Olivia was cut off by t giggles in the kitchen.

Will had never heard Jemmy giggle, and a lump formed in his throat. How had Emily, whom Jemmy had just met, broken through his nephew's paralyzing fears?

"Unka Weeoo!" Jemmy dashed into the living room, his face bright with an excitement Will had never seen. He stopped and stared at the adults, apparently forgetting Will wasn't the only one in the room.

Will had learned not to make sudden moves around Jemmy. Instead, he walked to the boy and knelt in front of him. "What is it, buddy? What did you see?"

Jemmy buried his face in Will's shoulder.

Emily skipped over to them. "Jemmy, Jemmy, come back. Mommy, it's the hummingbirds." She took Jemmy's hand and tugged...but gently. "C'mon, Jemmy," she coaxed.

Jemmy peeled himself slowly from Will's chest and let her lead him away, this time without a backward glance.

In that moment, Will knew he must make sure Jemmy had every opportunity to play with this precious little girl, no matter what it took.

Award-winning author **Louise M. Gouge** writes historical and contemporary fiction romances. She received the prestigious Inspirational Readers' Choice Award in 2005 and was a finalist in 2011, 2015, 2016 and 2017; was a finalist in the 2012 Laurel Wreath contest; and was a 2023 Selah Award finalist. Louise earned a BA in creative writing from the University of Central Florida and a master's of liberal studies degree from Rollins College. She taught English and humanities at Valencia College for sixteen and a half years and has written twenty-eight novels, eighteen of which were published under Harlequin's Love Inspired imprint. Contact Louise at louisemgougeauthor.blogspot.com, Facebook.com/LouiseMGougeAuthor and Twitter @louisemgouge.

Books by Louise M. Gouge

Love Inspired

Safe Haven Ranch

Love Inspired Historical

Finding Her Frontier Family
Finding Her Frontier Home

Four Stones Ranch

Cowboy to the Rescue
Cowboy Seeks a Bride
Cowgirl for Keeps
Cowgirl Under the Mistletoe
Cowboy Homecoming
Cowboy Lawman's Christmas Reunion

Visit the Author Profile page at LoveInspired.com for more titles.

Safe Haven Ranch

LOUISE M. GOUGE

LOVE INSPIRED
INSPIRATIONAL ROMANCE

LOVE INSPIRED®
INSPIRATIONAL ROMANCE

Recycling programs for this product may not exist in your area.

ISBN-13: 978-1-335-59736-6

Safe Haven Ranch

Copyright © 2024 by Louise M. Gouge

For questions and comments about the quality of this book, please contact us at CustomerService@Harlequin.com.

® is a trademark of Harlequin Enterprises ULC.

Love Inspired
22 Adelaide St. West, 41st Floor
Toronto, Ontario M5H 4E3, Canada
www.LoveInspired.com

Printed in Lithuania

MIX
Paper | Supporting responsible forestry
FSC® C021394

Pure religion and undefiled before God
and the Father is this, To visit the fatherless
and widows in their affliction, and to keep himself
unspotted from the world.
—*James* 1:27

My special thanks go to my wonderful agent,
Tamela Hancock Murray, and to my fabulous editor,
Shana Asaro, and her team, Rachel Burkot and
John Oberholtzer. You really made my book shine!
Thank you for all you do.

Also, thanks to my fellow author,
Debbie Lynne Costello, who provided research
into purebred dogs.

Finally, as with all of my stories, this book is
dedicated to my beloved husband, David,
my one and only love, who encouraged me
to write the stories of my heart and continued to
encourage me throughout my writing career.
David, I will always love you and miss you.

Chapter One

Outside Riverton, New Mexico
Late May

"You what?"

Olivia Ortiz stared at her elderly neighbor, barely sparing a glance at his too-handsome companion. "But, Albert, you promised to sell your land to me." She was standing in her own driveway, hands fisted at her waist in a defensive posture.

"I know, I know." Albert Winslow shrugged his bony shoulders and gave her an apologetic smile. "But wait 'til you hear what he has planned, and I think you'll like it. Will, how about you tell Miss Olivia what you have planned." As usual, the almost ninety-year-old gentleman repeated himself. He looked up at his much taller companion. "I think she'll like it."

"Um…" The younger man, who fit the very definition of a tall, dark and handsome cowboy—with curly black hair thrown in for good measure—grinned, and his blue eyes sparkled in the sunlight, causing a silly hiccup in Olivia's chest. "Don't you think you should introduce us first?"

"Oh." Albert blinked and looked from him to Olivia and back again. "Sure thing. Miss Olivia, this is Will Mattson.

Known this boy all his life. He's the grandson of my old friend Andy Mattson, Lord rest his soul. Will, this is Olivia Ortiz. She and her father own this property." He waved a hand around to include the fifteen acres that comprised her land, just over a quarter the size of his own fifty acres. Centered by matching pink adobe houses, the two properties were separated by a four-foot fieldstone fence, with a single flimsy, never-locked, much-used gate between them.

Will reached out a hand. "Pleased to meet you, ma'am." He gave her a wide smile, revealing perfect white teeth set off by his perfectly tanned complexion, which caused another hiccup near her heart.

What was wrong with her? She wasn't about to let herself fall for this man…or *any* man. No one could ever replace Sancho. Still, she briefly shook his hand as his name registered in her brain.

"Mattson? Are you…?" Annoyance replaced the shock that Albert's devastating news had delivered.

"Yes, ma'am." There went that cowboy "ma'am" thing again, punctuated by a boyish shuffling of his western boots on the dusty ground. "Can't escape it around here."

"Well, if you're a Mattson, why do you need this small property to add to the…what is it? Eight or ten thousand acres your family owns?" She didn't mean to sound so confrontational, but Albert had just crashed her desperately held dreams, so her social filters were crashing, too. "You plan to buy the whole county?"

"Unka Weeoo?" An adorable little brown-haired boy poked his head from behind the man's long legs. "Hokay?" His voice, barely above a whisper, wobbled, and his big blue eyes were round with fear.

How had Olivia failed to see the little guy? He must have been frightened by her outburst.

Will's expression became gentle, paternal. He scooped up the boy, who looked to be around four, and chucked him under the chin. "Sure thing, buddy. Everything's okay." He looked at Olivia. "This is Jemmy, my nephew."

"Hi, Jemmy." She swallowed a sudden lump in her throat. Her own son would be getting close to three, if only... She shook off the memory. "I have a daughter just about your age." Would six-year-old Emily be offended by being compared to a younger child? Olivia stopped short of asking the boy if he would like to meet Emily. That would seem like an invitation to these men to come inside.

Jemmy buried his face in Will's shoulder, then flung his arms around his uncle's neck.

"He's a little shy." Will gently massaged the boy's back.

What was the story there? Was Will babysitting? Olivia dismissed the questions. Her own question hadn't been answered. Why would a member of the wealthy Mattson family need Albert's property, set as it was in this little canyon beside the Rio Grande? It certainly wasn't enough land to run a herd of cattle, like on their other holdings. And she needed this land. It was her lifeline to restoring her very purpose in life, her only viable means of supporting herself and her daughter and giving them a future beyond what Sancho's life insurance provided. While Dad's pensions kept them afloat for now, he often reminded her that he wouldn't always be there for her.

"Why don't you invite us in for coffee," Albert said, "so I can say hello to your father." He took a step toward the back door to Olivia's house.

"I, uh..." She brushed a strand of sweat-dampened hair

from her forehead, then realized she'd probably streaked it with dirt. "I'm in the middle of planting these marigolds." She pointed to the line of prepared soil along the driveway. "The plants shouldn't lie out in the sun for long before going into the ground."

"Oh, come on, now." Albert took another step toward the house. "We won't be long, and I'd like to say hello to Lawrence."

She huffed out a harsh breath. When Albert got ahold of an idea, he didn't let go. Besides, this problem needed to be settled. *Now.* Maybe Dad could persuade Albert not to change his mind about the sale.

"Okay." *Not* okay. "Let's go in."

She led them through the long back room—a combination of library, reading room, office and model-train room—and into the living room.

"Have a seat." She waved a hand toward the couch and chairs set in a semicircle around the white adobe fireplace in the corner. "Dad, we have company," she called out. To her unwanted guests, she added, "I'll make coffee."

She went to the kitchen and washed the dirt from her hands, then tossed out the remnants of this morning's brew and washed the pot.

Emily skipped into the kitchen. "Did Mr. Albert come over?" She grabbed a paper napkin from the table and reached up to brush Olivia's forehead, sending a small shower of dirt to the floor. Sometimes it seemed Emily mothered Olivia as much as Olivia mothered her.

"Thank you, sweet pea. Yes, Mr. Albert and his friends." *His* friends. Not hers. "One of them is a little boy. Why don't you go see if he wants to play?" As she put a new filter into the coffee maker and measured the grounds, she nodded to the covered plate on the table. "And take them some of those sweet rolls we made this morning."

Emily danced over to the sink and washed her hands, not completely drying them, then gathered small plates and napkins and put them on a tray with the sweet rolls. If Olivia hadn't been so upset, she would burst with pride. Her daughter was already the perfect little hostess, which should go a long way in impressing their next client, who would soon be renting their studio apartment. People who rented the studio wanted peace and quiet, and might consider the presence of a child a big turnoff, but Emily could charm a grizzly bear.

"What's up, kiddo?" Dad limped into the kitchen, leaning on his ever-present quad-cane and looking older than his sixty-two years.

"It's—it's..." Olivia's eyes burned with sudden tears. She blinked them back. "Albert wants to sell his land to the Mattson family instead of us."

"What?" His tone was more curious than outraged, unlike what she'd felt upon hearing the news.

"He wants to explain it to me. To us."

She had to remember that this land actually belonged to Dad, although he always referred to it as *ours* and let her do what she wanted to the property. Seven years ago, Mom had inherited it from her parents, and she and Dad had moved here from Seattle. By then, Olivia and Sancho had been married, so she didn't live here until—she breathed out a sigh—Sancho had died over three years ago, and she'd come here so her parents could help her raise Emily. Then, last year, Mom died. Olivia swiped the back of her hand over the bothersome tears that ran down her cheeks at the memory. After such losses, would her grief ever subside?

"Huh." Dad started toward the living room. "I'll be interested in what he has to say."

In minutes, the coffeepot spat out its final drips. Olivia poured the fresh brew into an insulated carafe and set it on a tray, along with mugs, creamer and sugar.

In the living room, the men were already engaged in a lively conversation as they munched on the sweet rolls.

"Real tasty, as always." Albert took another bite.

"Yes, ma'am. Delicious." Will turned to Dad. "If you don't mind, Lawrence, I'd like to look at your model trains sometime." He accepted the steaming mug from Olivia. "Thanks, ma'am." He gave her a nod. "I think Jemmy will be real interested, too." With both hands occupied, he nudged the little boy with his elbow and smiled at him. "Won't you, buddy?"

Jemmy returned a round-eyed look, but didn't smile. They sure did look like a loving father and his son.

Olivia quickly quashed the thought. She wouldn't do herself any favors by admiring anything about this man.

"Sure thing." Dad beamed. "I'm always up for showing off my favorite hobby."

Olivia delivered the other mugs, then said in a stage whisper to Emily, "You can get juice boxes for you and Jemmy."

"Want to go with me?" Emily reached out a hand to the little boy.

As before, he buried himself in his uncle's protective embrace.

"It's okay, Jemmy." Again, Will's eyes exuded paternal kindness. "It's just in the other room. You can see me through the doorway. Wouldn't you like a juice box?"

Eyeing Emily with suspicion, Jemmy nonetheless scooted off the couch and, after a moment of hesitation, took her hand. She giggled and led him from the room in her older-sister way, as she always did with younger kids. Jemmy looked back at Will but didn't tug against her grip.

As he watched them, Will released a quiet sigh. "Thanks."

Olivia tried to subdue the empathy welling up inside her. Was he raising this child?

"Now, let's get down to business," Albert said, interrupting her thoughts. "Will, how about you tell Olivia and Lawrence about your plans. I think they're going to like them."

Olivia couldn't quite school her face into a polite expression, but Dad's interest was clear from his raised eyebrows, to his half smile, to his posture as he leaned toward their guest. But then, Dad was always friendly and interested in other people, even if they might not return the attitude.

Will shifted in his seat at the end of the couch. "Well, it's something I've been praying about for some time."

Oh, great. That makes it sound like God's already on your side.

"Albert's land, being tucked away in this little valley, would be the perfect location for my plans." He gave Olivia that white-toothed smile that probably charmed all the girls in Riverton and parts beyond. "I'd like to establish a boys' ranch for at-risk younger boys, away from the negative influences of their present lives. You know, kids who maybe come from abusive homes or have parents or older siblings who've chosen the wrong path. These boys need some foundation to their lives so they won't follow that same pattern. My aunt fosters four boys right now and wants to take on more, but her house and yard in town aren't big enough. I want to give her a home that is. And, of course, I'll live there, too."

Olivia felt as if a boulder had slammed against her chest, while her heart sank deeper with each word. Sancho had worked with troubled teens, and he'd been murdered for it. And this man wanted to buy the land that should be hers and bring a bunch of troublemakers to live on the next property, all too close to Emily. Added to that, a noisy herd of wild boys would destroy the peace and quiet she promised to her prospective clients. Who would come here for a quiet retreat from the world, only to be met with screaming, shouting kids?

"Isn't that a fine plan, Olivia?" Albert gave her a big smile.

Even Dad looked at her expectantly. Didn't he see the obvious problem? Time to address the foundational issue.

"I'm sure Mr. Mattson is sincere in his desire to help troubled children, but this isn't the place for it." She worked hard to keep the resentment from her voice. From Dad's frown, she could see she wasn't succeeding. "Albert, you are an old-school gentleman, and we both subscribe to old-fashioned values. When you agreed to sell your land to me, I took that as a firm commitment from you—a handshake, if you will, which to us is as unbreakable as a written contract."

Silence filled the living room, broken only by the sounds from the kitchen, where Emily chattered to Jemmy about the various flavors of juice in the refrigerator. What a wonderful big sister she would have made to little Daniel. But Sancho's death had traumatized Olivia, and she'd miscarried at six months.

Her husband, her son, her mother. How many more losses would the Lord send into her life? Must she also give up the dream that had begun to restore her mental and emotional health, and most of all, her faith? Add to that her financial needs, and she was determined to hold Albert to his word.

No, this deal must not go through. She had to do everything in her power to persuade Albert to keep his promise. But what power did she actually have?

As if showing her the way, her spine stiffened, and she sat up straighter.

"Albert, you know a gang of delinquent kids murdered my husband. I can't let the same kind of criminals take my livelihood, too, not to mention threaten Emily's safety."

A stinging buzz streaked up Will's neck and raised the hair on his scalp. Wow. Just wow. Albert had told him Olivia Ortiz was a widow, but he hadn't said her husband had been murdered. And by gang members. No wonder she didn't like his plan. More like hated it, actually. What should he say now? Offer his condolences for her loss? Point out that his boys wouldn't be violent? And what was that about her livelihood?

Lord, I know You've brought me to this place. What should I say now?

"Man, I'm so sorry to hear about your husband." The words came out without further thought. "I can't imagine…"

He shut up before he stuck his foot in his mouth. When his sister died violently last year, he'd been devastated. Nothing anybody said had consoled him, and a few "friends" blamed her for sticking with that creep… *Sorry, Lord—* that abusive, narcissistic alcoholic she'd married despite the family's pleas. In spite of their own sad history, with Mom leaving when they were kids, Megan always thought she could fix things and people. Clearly, she hadn't succeeded with Ed. After he killed her, he barricaded himself in a motel room and was shot by a SWAT marksman who didn't realize Jemmy was also in the room. It had been six months since that shootout, and Jemmy still had nightmares.

"It's a rough world out there." Albert reached over and patted Olivia's hand. "But we can still do some good in our little corner, can't we? That's why I liked Will's idea so much."

Her wounded look moved Will, and she seemed on the verge of tears. The urge to comfort her came on strong, but he forced it back. Being too empathetic with some women could give the wrong impression, maybe even get him in trouble…again. Best to ignore her emotions and discuss only the facts of this matter. Of course, she'd looked pretty cute with that swipe of dirt on her forehead. She must have looked in a mirror and washed it off while she was in the kitchen.

Nope. Not going to think about her that way. That just leads to trouble.

"Ma'am, I'd be interested in hearing more about your plans. Albert tells me you've been hosting authors and artists in your studio apartment. How will you use his house?"

She cleared her throat and sniffed back the tears, settling a blank expression on her pretty face. *Stop that, you doofus. You can't think of her as pretty. It can only lead to trouble*—heart *trouble.*

"I plan to expand my business and make room for more artists who need a quiet place to express their art. A safe refuge from fans whose interruptions can destroy concentration, not to mention inspiration." Her expression softened as she warmed to her topic. "As Albert may have told you, these two properties were settled in the early 1900s by artistic women who were searching for that very thing. They supported each other and explored opportunities not available in the outside world during that era. I plan to carry on that tradition for this land." She laughed softly, a pleasing, musical sound. "Of course, things have improved for women since then, but artists still need peace and quiet when they're trying to write that next big novel or paint that glorious landscape. We're highly selective in our clientele, all of whom hear of us by word of mouth from their friends."

She sounded like a brochure for the place, but from what she'd said, she clearly didn't advertise.

"Tell them who's coming today, Olivia." Lawrence's dark eyes flared with excitement. "None other than *New York Times* bestseller Nona—"

"Dad!" Olivia glared at him. "We never share who'll be staying here. Privacy. Obnoxious fans. Remember?"

"Oops." He laughed, clearly not embarrassed by her scolding. He turned to Will. "You get the idea, right?"

"Yes, sir." Indeed he did. More than that, he understood the need for privacy. All his life, people—especially women—had expectations of him because his name was Mattson. Despite Will being only ten years old when Mom left, Dad had expected him to be stoic, claiming a Mattson didn't give in to emotions. Then, after Will's last girlfriend had made clear she would expect a pampered, jet-set life as Mrs. Will Mattson, he'd decided to stop dating. Instead, he spent his energy and resources helping boys who had no agenda beyond wanting and needing love, a full stomach and a clean bed. Some of them needed a home where disreputable relatives couldn't find them and use them for selfish or even evil purposes. Boys like Jemmy. So far, Ed's relatives hadn't come up with any legal reason for claiming custody, but they'd made plenty of noise and threats.

So, understanding aside, he had to fight for the right to buy Albert's property. While he valued the man's promise to Olivia, he knew this area well, and not a single plot

of land provided what this remote fifty-acre riverside valley did.

"Miss Olivia?" He gave her a gentle smile just short of
pouring on the infamous Mattson charm. "I really need
this land. A bunch of disadvantaged boys are counting on
it. Won't you please release Albert from his promise to sell
it to you?"

Confusion crossed her face. Then she lifted her chin and
glared at him. "You mean you aren't going to call in your
lawyers and claim a verbal contract doesn't count legally?"

He chuckled. "No, ma'am. I'm a lawyer myself—family
law—but I don't believe in using the law to bully people."
He glanced at Albert, who was closely watching the interaction. "I've found the best way to handle situations like
this is through prayer and healthy arbitration, so everybody comes out of it believing the right thing's been done."

She blinked those dark brown eyes, and her jaw dropped.
"Prayer?" She looked at her dad, then back at Will. "Do you
say that so you can claim God is on your side?"

Will rocked back in his seat. "Uh, no, not at all. Just the
opposite. I pray to learn God's will, even if it's not what I've
asked for."

"Oh, I see. So—"

Olivia's frosty response was cut off by the sound of giggles in the kitchen, and not just from little Emily. It was a
beautiful duet of lighthearted noise from two kids clearly
having innocent fun. Will had never heard Jemmy giggle,
and a lump formed in his throat. How had Emily, whom
Jemmy had just met, broken through his nephew's paralyzing fears and caused such carefree laughter when his
young cousins hadn't been able to?

"Unka Weeoo!" Jemmy dashed into the living room,

his face bright with an excitement Will had never seen. He stopped and stared at the adults, apparently forgetting Will wasn't the only one in the room. His face clouded, and his thumb went into his mouth.

Will stood slowly. He'd learned not to make sudden moves around Jemmy. Instead, he walked to the boy and kneeled in front of him. "What is it, buddy? What did you see?"

Jemmy buried his face in Will's shoulder.

Emily skipped over to them. "Jemmy, Jemmy, come back. Mommy, it's the hummingbirds. They came back to the feeder." She took Jemmy's hand and tugged, but gently. "C'mon, Jemmy," she coaxed. "You'll miss it. And we need to make more sugar water for them."

Jemmy peeled himself slowly from Will's chest and let her lead him away, this time without a backward glance.

In that moment, Will knew one thing. He must make sure Jemmy had every opportunity to play with this precious little girl, no matter what it took.

Chapter Two

"**W**hat time does Nona's plane land? You don't want to be late." Their company had left, and Dad was helping Olivia clear the coffee table and carry the mugs and plates to the kitchen.

"Two o'clock." Olivia opened the dishwasher and began to load it. "I have plenty of time. Just need to finish planting the marigolds or we're going to lose them. If I'd known Albert and his friend were going to interrupt me, I wouldn't have taken them out of their starter pots."

"I can finish the planting." Contrary to his words, Dad plunked himself down at the kitchen table.

Olivia glanced his way, worry niggling into her thoughts. Over a year ago, he'd been crushed by Mom's death, and despite his love for her and Emily, sometimes he seemed to lose his interest in life. Maybe letting him plant the flowers would be good.

"Okay. Thanks. Just be sure to—" She stopped. It was okay if he planted them in a crooked row. Sancho always teased her about her insistence on perfection, whether decorating a cake or planting annuals along the front walkway of their Seattle home. "I think they'll need a little water."

"Sure thing." He shuffled the salt and pepper shakers

like chess pieces, his usual habit when he had something on his mind.

"You want to talk?" She closed the dishwasher and went to the fridge to gather lunch fixings.

"That Will Mattson seems like a decent fellow." Dad didn't look her way. "Can't help but admire him for wanting to help kids and get them out of bad situations."

Her heart and mind still reeling from Albert's request, Olivia pulled out a chair across the table from him and sat. "So, does that mean you want Albert to sell *him* the land?"

"No." Dad shook his head and gave her a scolding look. "You don't have to take off in that direction." Then he chuckled. "Was just thinking he's about your age. Single. Christian. And—"

"And that's enough of that." She stood and returned to the lunch prep, putting together sandwiches. Rather, slapping them together was more like it. When had Dad decided she was interested in forming a romantic relationship? Did she hassle him to respond to the widows at church who tried to get his attention? No way. She and Emily had a good life here with him. Why would they need to add anyone to their family? Especially not a rich, land-grabbing cowboy who was trying to destroy her dreams.

"So this rich guy plans to outbid you on the land deal?" Nona Albright sat in the passenger seat of Olivia's Explorer as they drove north from Santa Fe Regional Airport.

The moment Olivia had met the fifty-something author at baggage claim, they'd bonded over books, horses, purses and shoes. Nona broke the stereotype of the introverted writer. She'd managed to extract the story of Olivia's land dilemma within their first half hour.

"Well, not exactly." After a brief glance at her guest, Olivia kept her eyes on the winding four-lane highway toward home. "He just suggested we pray about it." Why was she defending the man who was out to steal her dream?

"Huh." Nona checked her appearance in the sun-visor mirror. "If he's for real, that speaks highly of him. But some people use prayer as a tool to manipulate others."

"Like Arnett in your last novel."

Nona laughed. "Yes. I created that character from a real-life charmer I once knew."

"I can't wait to read your next book. When will it be released?"

Nona laughed again, a pleasant alto chuckle. "If I don't get it written, it won't release at all. My publisher had to push up my deadline. Hence my need for this getaway. My house is chaos central. So, when my older daughter offered to stay home with my teenage one, three dogs and more cats than I can count, I couldn't pass it up." She reached over and patted Olivia's hand. "I'm so glad you had an opening. Ina told me what a wonderful hostess you are and how beautiful and quiet your little ranch is."

Quiet for now. If Will Mattson got his way, it would turn into the Wild West. But she shouldn't drag Nona into her conflict. "I owe Ina big-time for giving me this idea. It's lots of fun to meet such talented people."

"And I look forward to meeting your dad and daughter. Lawrence and Emily, right?"

"Right." How thoughtful of her to remember their names, which Olivia might have mentioned a single time during their phone conversations as they arranged Nona's stay.

She turned off the highway and onto the first of several unmarked dirt roads leading to her ranch. A person had to know where they were going out here or they would end up lost—another reason she had to buy Albert's land. Only the small local communities knew about their two properties tucked away from civilization, and most of them valued their privacy as much as Olivia valued hers.

The final turn led to the road past Albert's property and then close to the fifteen-foot-high berm that protected the little valley from the Rio Grande's springtime flooding. A canopy of aspen and cottonwood trees arched over the rutted road, their abundant green leaves waving a welcome in the breeze. One final turn, and they were facing the gate to her property. Beyond the barbed wire and slatted fence sat her pink adobe house. She glanced at Nona, whose eyes were bright with appreciation.

"It's beautiful. Just what I imagined." Nona released her seat belt. "I'll get the gate." She was out of the car before Olivia could object. How nice that this client wouldn't require pampering.

They drove around the house to the door of the attached studio apartment, and Olivia helped Nona carry her suitcases and laptop inside. On her trip back to the car, she saw her guest staring across the fieldstone fence and followed her gaze.

To her surprise and annoyance, Will—with shirtsleeves rolled up to show off his tanned, muscular arms—was chopping wood beside Albert's long-neglected woodpile. Chopping wood in May, a month in which most people didn't even use their fireplaces. What was that all about?

"Oh, my." Nona glanced at Olivia. "Tell me that's not your rich land grabber." She laughed. "Or tell me he is, and introduce us."

"Um, yes, but—"

"Just kidding." Nona nudged Olivia's shoulder. "He's more than a little too young for me."

Olivia's answering smile felt more like a grimace. Was there a hint of matchmaking in Nona's sideways glance? Did the suspense writer have a hint of romance writer in her? *Please, no.*

Inside the apartment, Nona surveyed the large room's furnishings. "Oh, this is just great. Cute little kitchenette. Treadmill. Desk. And I adore your Southwestern decor." She brushed a hand over the orange, red, yellow and brown woolen throw draped over the back of the love seat. "I may have to change the setting for my book from eastern city to southwest ranch." Her laughter showed she was joking.

After a little more chitchat, Olivia excused herself. "I have to make the cornbread for supper. Is chili still okay?" They'd discussed food preferences over the phone, and Olivia had stocked up on Nona's favorites.

"Sounds good."

While she and Emily whipped up the cornbread, Olivia couldn't put aside thoughts of her dilemma. In truth, Will's suggestion that they should pray about the land situation had brought on some guilt.

Her prayer life had suffered after Sancho's cruel death, but after an inspiring sermon by her parents' pastor, who'd suffered his own losses, she'd started taking baby steps to restore her faith. Dad had reminded her that Emily needed to hear about Jesus, to *see* Jesus in her and in him before other voices caught her attention. Homeschooling her daughter with faith-based kindergarten materials helped. And now, she'd already registered for a homeschooling convention in July so she could purchase the best first-grade curriculum. She hoped those lessons would give Emily the spiritual instruction she needed.

As far as Emily seeing Jesus in her, well, she tried... until situations came up like the one today. How was she supposed to react kindly to someone who was trying to steal her dream of self-sufficiency? Until now, the Lord seemed to have paved the way for her to achieve that dream. Why would He throw this roadblock into her plans? More than a roadblock, it was a demolition. Didn't He care that she needed Albert's land so she could provide for Emily? Renting the studio to one client at a time didn't bring in enough income, and if Dad continued to decline, his pensions might need to go toward senior living arrangements sooner rather than later. She couldn't bear that thought, but she'd learned the hard way life often sent unexpected disappointments and tragedies.

She didn't realize her eyes had filled with tears until Emily hugged her waist.

"I love you, Mommy." The concern in her brown eyes melted Olivia's heart. Her daughter had such gentle, empathetic ways.

Olivia forced a light laugh to ease Emily's mind. "I love you, too. Let's get this cornbread in the oven." She scraped the last of the golden mixture into the cast-iron skillet, shoved it into the oven and set the timer.

"Mommy, I like Jemmy." Olivia started setting the table without being asked. "Is he coming to supper?"

"No, sweet pea. Our guest is Miss Nona."

"Speaking of whom..." Dad entered the kitchen, freshly cleaned up from planting the marigolds in a better line than Olivia had expected. "I'll be happy to tell her it's ready."

"Um...okay." Olivia knew he enjoyed reading Nona's thriller novels. "Don't go all fanboy on her."

"Humph." He feigned an indignant expression. "I may ask for an autograph in my books, but I'll keep it cool."

"Grampy, I like Jemmy," Emily said, grabbing his hand and repeating what she'd said to Olivia. Repetition meant this was important to her, so Olivia paid attention.

"You do?" Dad tweaked Emily's nose, which brought on the usual giggles.

"Yes, sir. Can I play with him again?"

Dad glanced at Olivia. "That's up to your mom, honey."

Olivia's heart sank. She was so careful about which children she allowed into her daughter's life. Jemmy seemed needy but harmless, though letting Emily play with him meant contact with Will. Yet how could she refuse?

She couldn't. Which meant this situation was just getting worse and worse.

Will checked on Jemmy, who was napping on Albert's couch, then returned to the kitchen to find something for supper. The nearly bare cupboard and fridge revealed Albert had been eating mostly eggs gathered from his dozen or so hens. Not the worst diet, but not the best, either. No wonder Albert's grandson wanted him to sell the land and move to Amarillo to live with his family.

The run-down look of the house was more cosmetic than structural, although it could use a new roof over the south bedrooms. The outbuildings could use some reinforcement and...

And Will wouldn't be making any of those improvements if Mrs. Ortiz had her way. For a moment in her living room, the lawyer in him had been tempted to ask who actually owned the place, who actually had the funds to buy Albert's property. Lawrence seemed to like Will's plans for a boys' ranch, but he'd let his daughter lead the conversation. After pondering his approach, Will knew he couldn't, in good conscience, come between father and daughter any more than he could ask Albert to break his word to his pretty next-door neighbor.

When he and Albert had left her house, he had to admit his usual optimism had taken a hit. So, he and Albert had brainstormed ideas to persuade her to change her mind. Nothing aboveboard and workable came up. In the meantime, Will could see Albert needed someone to move in and take care of him. Until such a person could be found, Will knew he had to stay. He'd already put his law practice into his cousin Sam's capable hands while he made his plans for the ranch, so he was free to do whatever it took to help Albert.

So, today he'd done some serious cleanup, both inside and out. He'd gotten a little out of shape, so it felt good to chop the wood and straighten the woodpile. Jemmy had taken seriously his job of stacking the cut logs. Never mind that Will had to restack them and remove a couple of splinters from the little guy's hand. Then they'd cleaned up the kitchen. No telling how long it had been since Albert had washed dishes.

And now, Will needed to figure out some supper for the old man, plus himself and Jemmy. The only item in the freezer was an unidentifiable, foil-wrapped block. Even if it was something edible, it was too late to thaw it. He'd have to go to town, but that might take too long. Jemmy would be hungry soon.

Only one solution to this problem. Even if it meant

breaking one of his own rules about leaving the boy, especially when he was sleeping.

"Albert, would you watch Jemmy while I run an errand? If he wakes up, you can turn on cartoons." He nodded toward the television.

"Sure thing." Albert settled into a chair in the living room and picked up a book from the side table. "Take your time. We'll be fine. If something comes up, I have my cell phone right here." He held up the device.

"I won't be long."

The trip across the broad yards between the two houses took less than a minute. Will walked through the gate and around to the front door and knocked. When Mrs. Ortiz opened the door, his heart did an odd little flip. She sure was pretty in her jeans and peach T-shirt, even with suspicion filling her brown eyes.

"Yes?" She sounded guarded, of course.

He'd like to reassure her that he meant her no harm, but he had to stick to his mission.

"Mrs. Ortiz—"

"Olivia." She spoke her name as an order, which made him smile.

"Yes, ma'am. Olivia. I come to you with figurative hat in hand. Albert doesn't have much in the way of food in his house, and it's getting past suppertime. Do you…?"

"Oh, no." Alarm filled her face. "Yes, of course. I usually take something over for him every day, but I've been so busy." She huffed out a breath. "No excuses. Yes, of course." She glanced toward the kitchen. "We have plenty. Why don't you bring him over, and I'll give him dinner. And you, as well." She grimaced as though those last words tasted bad.

He chuckled. "You don't have to feed me, but I would appreciate a peanut-butter sandwich for Jemmy."

"Don't be silly. If you're helping Albert, I can feed you. Chili, cornbread, salad, sweet tea. Carrot cake for dessert. Dinner's in fifteen minutes." She shut the door before he could respond.

Carrot cake? Sounded good. He couldn't wait to try it. He chuckled all the way back to Albert's. Just as he'd thought, she had a kind heart. He'd seen it in the way she'd looked at Jemmy that morning. To know she often fed Albert only added to her appeal.

Appeal? What was he thinking? He couldn't let a pretty woman get under his skin and deter him from his plans. Especially not one who seemed insistent on standing in his way of making a home for his boys. He shouldn't worry, though. Miss Olivia had nothing in common with the women who usually tried to get his attention. In fact, if he wasn't so set on staying single, her brusque, standoffish manner might have hurt his manly pride just a tad. As it was, they had a mutual lack of interest in each other, which suited him just fine.

When he woke Jemmy and told him about their supper plans, his nephew grinned like Will had never seen before.

"I can play with Em'ly."

The brightness in his eyes almost made Will tear up. Somehow, he managed to answer.

"Yep. And eat supper, too."

"Olivia makes a mean chili." Albert seemed as eager as Jemmy. "And melt-in-your-mouth cornbread."

It sounded good to Will, but it wasn't until they entered the other house and caught the enticing aromas that his mouth began to water and his belly rumbled with hunger.

* * *

Years ago, Olivia had found her gift in extending hospitality. Nothing gave her more personal satisfaction than having company, giving them a comfortable bed and feeding them a delicious meal. Mom had set the example by frequently having guests. And Olivia and Sancho had often invited the elderly or church newcomers over for a meal after services. That was why Ina's idea about hosting artists had appealed to her enough to propel her into her present business.

And that was why feeding Albert had come naturally. It had been during one of his supper visits that they'd discussed her purchasing his land, and he'd said he would sell it to her. And now, that promise, as fragile as the old gentleman, was in danger of being canceled. She still didn't trust Will Mattson not to pull some lawyer trick to change Albert's mind, maybe even confuse the poor old man. No, that wasn't fair. Albert might be slowing down physically, but his mind was still sharp.

When he arrived with Will and Jemmy, Dad, Nona and Emily were waiting in the living room. Emily skipped over to Jemmy and took his hand. His cute grin brought a smile to Olivia's lips. After she made introductions, they proceeded into the dining room. The kids sat at Emily's little table off to the side, and Olivia permitted herself a bittersweet moment as she pictured the son she'd lost sitting with them.

"My, oh, my, Olivia." Albert settled into his chair beside Nona. "I could smell your fine cooking halfway here. Bring it on."

Olivia laughed with the others as she carried the large earthenware serving bowl to the table, but her heart ached for her friend. She'd been so alarmed by what he'd said in his earlier visit that she failed to notice how frail he looked. In a moment of panic, she wondered if chili might upset his stomach, but he didn't appear at all worried.

Dad offered his usual beautiful prayer, thanking the Lord for His provision and for good friends to share it with. Then he stood and served out bowls of chili while Olivia passed the salad and cornbread. Everybody dug in and quickly offered high praise.

"'Scuse me, ma'am." After his first bite, Will cast a look of concern toward the kids. "This is mighty tasty, but are they having this same chili?"

"No, of course not." Olivia tried not to sound defensive but failed. From the other end of the table, Dad gave a little shake of his head, so she modified her tone. "The cornbread's the same, but I always make a milder chili for Emily. If you prefer, I could take it away and make Jemmy a PB and J."

Hearing his name, Jemmy looked her way, and his eyes grew round. He turned his startled look to Will.

"It's okay, buddy. Do you like the chili?"

He answered with a nod, then hunched protectively over the bowl and took another bite.

"Sorry," Will whispered. "His dad used food as discipline, so sometimes he's scared his food will be taken away. We're working through that."

Olivia couldn't swallow the bite she'd just taken, so she washed it down with her iced tea. What kind of person could be so cruel to any child, much less his own? She glanced at the other end of the table, where Dad, Nona and Albert were deep into their own conversation.

"So, you're gonna finish the series up with this one?"

Dad's interest in their guest hadn't reached fanboy level yet, to Olivia's relief, but he did seem extra friendly toward her.

Nona dabbed her lips with her napkin. "That's the plan." She smiled, and her amber eyes twinkled. "What do you think should happen to bring it all to a close?"

Dad chuckled. "Oh, no. I'm not going to tamper with genius. You just keep writing like you've been doing."

"So, you're a writer?" Will's expression exuded sincerity, but Olivia had her doubts. Who in the world hadn't heard of Nona Albright?

Nona, however, didn't seem offended by the question. "I am."

"And a brilliant one, too," Dad said. "I'll loan you one of her books. I have them all."

"And that's enough about me." Nona turned to Albert. "Tell me about you. How long have you lived here? And what can you tell me about the women who settled here in the early 1900s? I may need to write a book about them."

Albert beamed. "Ah. One of my favorite subjects. One of those women was my great-grandmother. I grew up right here." He took a bite of cornbread, but she was still looking at him expectantly. After he swallowed, he said, "I can show you her diaries, if you like."

"Oh, that would be wonderful," Nona said. "But tell me more about what it was like growing up here."

"All right." Albert chuckled. "When I was a boy, my folks started a birthday tradition for me. I was born on July fourth, so they started having a big party for me. Invited folks from the local communities. It grew into an annual Independence Day celebration." He looked at Olivia. "And that gives me an idea."

"Great." Olivia wasn't sure she trusted whatever he was

going to say, although last year, she and Emily had loved his Fourth of July celebration. "Let me serve dessert, then you can tell us."

She and Nona cleared the table, and Olivia brought out her homemade carrot cake. After everybody was served and began to eat, Will hummed his appreciation.

"Wow, this is my first carrot cake ever, and it's now officially my new favorite dessert."

Olivia rolled her eyes. "Right." She focused on Albert. "Okay, what's your idea?"

"Oh, you're gonna like this. I've hosted that celebration for close to ninety years, give or take a few. But I'm just not sure I can do it again." His pale blue eyes took in both her and Will. "I'm gonna need some help so I can go out with a bang."

"Sure. Glad to help." Will, seated across from Albert, leaned forward. "What can I do?"

"Well, I spent this afternoon considering some ideas for making things work for both you and Olivia in this land situation." He winked at Olivia, and her heart dropped. This couldn't be good. "I want the two of you to have a competition. I'll assign responsibilities to each of you, and whoever does the best job gets to make the final decision about who buys my place."

Nona's attention was riveted on the discussion. "How will you decide who does the best job? They both appear to be very capable people."

Albert frowned. "Hadn't thought that far."

"How about letting the folks who attend cast ballots?" Dad grinned at Olivia, who returned a frown. What was he thinking by contributing to this wild scheme?

"What a great idea." Nona gave Olivia a conspiratorial wink. "Let me know if I can help."

"Sounds good to me," Will said.

"What do you think, Olivia?" Albert's excitement was obvious from the way he bounced in his seat with boyish enthusiasm.

All she could do was offer a shaky smile as her heart sank even lower. Will would probably bring in a bunch of his relatives to vote for him. She didn't have a posse to help her out, so he would no doubt win this silly competition. And, of course, he would choose to buy the land, then once he moved in with those noisy boys, she might as well kiss her hospitality business goodbye.

Chapter Three

"This celebration is going to be fun." Nona had insisted on helping Olivia clean up after supper and had an instinct for where to put items she cleared from the dining-room table. "I'm glad I'll be here for it. And I really like your cowboy. He sure is an old-fashioned gentleman."

Olivia cringed inwardly, but she didn't want to alienate her guest by arguing about her nemesis. She glanced through the doorway into the living room, where Dad chatted with Albert and Will, and the kids played with Emily's LEGO blocks on the rug in front of the fireplace.

"Yes, he seems quite the hero. A knight in shining armor." She wiped out the cast-iron skillet with a paper towel and put it on the back burner of the gas stove, where it would be ready for tomorrow's breakfast bacon. "I can just see him on the cover of a romance novel." She didn't care for most romance novels, so thinking of him that way put some distance between her rational brain and her silly, involuntary reactions to him.

As Nona brushed off the place mats over the sink, she laughed. "Hmm. There's an idea. I'm going to jot down a few observations about him. Maybe my next book after this one will be a romance."

Uh-oh. Best to change the subject. "So, where do you get your ideas?"

Again, Nona laughed. "That's the question people ask me most often. I grew up on Nancy Drew and in high school moved on to Agatha Christie, so I was always fascinated by suspense and mysteries, especially in real life. Just about anything can set me off on a creative tangent. For instance, as we drove here from the airport, I saw two intriguing things that set my creative juices flowing. Wrote them down as soon as I got unpacked."

"Wow. Though I shouldn't be too surprised. That's the way I am with recipes."

"Now, about this Independence Day, aka Albert's birthday celebration. What are we going to do?"

We? Nona's willingness to jump in and help surprised her.

"Good question. I assume I'll manage the food." Olivia had only attended the event one time—last year—when she'd finally tried to reclaim some sort of normal life after Sancho's death. "Maybe a cake-decorating competition? An old-fashioned cakewalk? Grilled hamburgers and all the fixings, for sure." She dried her hands on a tea towel and punched the start button on the dishwasher. "What do you think?"

"It helps to know your audience. Who usually comes? How many? Mainly children, or adults, too?"

Wow, Nona's creative mind sure was humming with ideas. "Families. All ages. Albert limits the invitation to the local communities to keep it under control. Local neighbors and friends from the San Juan area. Maybe a hundred to a hundred and fifty people."

"Fireworks?"

"No, those are not allowed. The area's had too many forest fires to risk it. When conditions are safe, he does let the kids have sparklers...under strict control."

"Ah. Very sensible."

Olivia sighed. "It's the only day of the year when Albert's place gets noisy, so I hope you won't be bothered."

"That's over a month away, so I'm sure I'll be far enough along with my word count to take a day off." Nona turned her attention to the door and smiled.

And there stood Dad, his eyes on Nona. Again, she wondered, what was that all about?

"Say, Livy," Dad said. "If you're done in here, come on in the other room and let's talk. Albert has some more ideas."

Oh, great. More nails in my coffin. "Sure. Coming right away."

Once she settled in her favorite chair—and noticed Dad making a place for Nona beside him on the couch—she turned her attention to Albert and did her best to ignore Will. Did he realize the black curls across his broad, tanned forehead made him even more attractive? Did he arrange them that way on purpose? *Oh, stop that!*

"I'm coming up with more ideas." Albert's wide smile revealed his perfect dentures *and* his excitement. "Will was saying he'd manage the games, but I have a better idea. I think he should manage the food, and Olivia should manage the games. That way you're both doing something new, that you aren't already familiar with. What do you think?"

"Sounds good to me," Will said. "I'll bring over a side of beef and cook it on an open pit." He winked at Olivia, which sent an odd little tickle through her middle. "We Mattsons are known for our barbecue beef."

"Oh, well, then." Albert gave him a wily grin. "Olivia will provide the beef. I'll pay for it, of course. And you can manage the rest of the food."

"Oh, no." Will leaned back, rolled his eyes and laughed. "You sure do plan to make it hard on us, don't you? All right, then. I'm game. Olivia?"

She was already scrambling in her mind for the best barbecue recipe. Nothing came up. Her specialty was baking. For barbecue, she'd always bought bottles of Sancho's favorite sauce, and lately that seemed to suit Dad, too. But store-bought sauce did not line the path to victory. It would take some serious internet research to find the right way to prepare an entire side of beef.

"If I may jump in here." Nona's eyes were bright with interest. "What would you think if I set up a book-signing booth? I can have my daughter send me some boxes of my backlist, and I can sell them at a big discount. All the proceeds will go to your favorite charity."

"That's mighty generous, Miss Nona." Dad patted her hand. "I can help you."

"Great." She returned his smile. "And I'm going to send Ina a text to see if she wants to come and have a sketch booth. She used to do sketches for a living at a Florida theme park before her painting career took off."

"My, oh, my." Albert slapped the arm of his chair. "This just gets better and better."

Olivia gave him a strained smile. In the midst of all these fine plans for joining his birthday with a grand Independence Day celebration, everybody seemed to forget that she was in danger of losing not only her dream, but also her very means of supporting herself and her daughter.

As Will drove his Chevy Silverado back toward Riverton, he shot a quick glance at the rearview mirror to check on Jemmy, who was strapped in his booster chair in the back seat. He'd never seen the little guy happy or laughing, so today had been a blessing beyond measure. From the first moment Emily took his hand, she'd treated him like he was her best friend. His Mattson cousins, of whom there were many, had also tried to befriend him, but their roughhousing and wrestling had frightened Jemmy, probably reminding him of Ed's abuse.

As for Olivia, while she obviously had no interest in befriending Will, she was kind and gentle with Jemmy. He could see a nurturing personality in her pretty brown eyes.

He chuckled as he recalled her alarm at Albert's suggestion about the competition. While she hadn't changed her mind about her so-called *right* to buy the property, she'd surrendered to the Independence Day plans, probably because of Nona's enthusiasm. And her father's. Lawrence sure was a generous, laid-back guy. He'd shown Jemmy his model train setup, and Jemmy stared at it with mild curiosity. But when Lawrence offered him an engineer's hat, he'd withdrawn again. Maybe next time.

And maybe next time, he could offer an olive branch to try to win Olivia's friendship, if not her agreement to release Albert from his promise.

A jackrabbit dashed across the road, and Will barely managed to stomp the brakes to keep from hitting it. "Whoa. That was close." *Better quit daydreaming.*

"Whoa!" Jemmy echoed. Another glance in the mirror revealed alarm on the boy's face.

"It's okay, buddy. Uncle Will's got this."

"Unka Weeoo go' dis."

Will swallowed the sudden lump in his throat. Jemmy's growing trust in him meant a lot, and he would do everything in his power not to disappoint the little guy. Or the four other little guys Aunt Lila Rose fostered, boys from seven to nine years old from dysfunctional families, each with special issues, the main one being the need for security. In addition to nurturing Will after Mom left, his aunt had been a foster mom for years after her own two children had grown up, which had inspired him to take the state-mandated courses to qualify as a foster parent himself. Together, they worked hard to let each boy know someone was watching out for them. It usually worked. Jemmy just needed more time with them.

After stopping at Walmart to pick up food and other items needed for survival at Albert's place, he drove to his aunt's wood-frame house in suburban Riverton. As always, the boys clamored for his attention, which caused Jemmy to withdraw to a corner of the couch and suck his thumb. Will didn't yet know how to help him get over this behavior, but he wouldn't force it.

He distributed the usual popcorn treats, mindful of Aunt Lila Rose's limitations on sweets at bedtime, and read to them a chapter from *The Lord of the Rings*. After reading time, he tucked each one into bed, listened to their chatter and their prayers, then returned to the living room, where his aunt was sitting with Jemmy.

"How long will you be at Albert's?" she asked. "Are you sure you don't want me to keep Jemmy?"

Alarm filled Jemmy's eyes, so Will squeezed his shoulder.

"No. I can't get by without my little buddy." He winked at his aunt, and she returned an understanding nod. "We'll probably stay until after the Fourth of July. I expect Albert to move to Amarillo after that. But I'll come by here every evening and read to the boys."

"That's good. They really look forward to your coming."

After a quick trip to his apartment to pack their bags, he and Jemmy drove back to Albert's. The rutted dirt roads weren't easy to navigate, especially in the dark, but he managed to find the almost hidden signposts along the way, thanks to his truck's elevation and high beams. Sometimes the light caught the startled look of coyotes or mule deer, or the rare peccary beside the road, which reminded him to take care as he drove. Too many lives had been lost in this area after wild Saturday-night parties. Two little brothers in Aunt Lila Rose's care had lost their parents that way only last Christmas. Will's constant prayer was that he could make a difference in their lives and steer them to a healthier lifestyle than their parents had indulged in.

Seeing a large, shadowy shape beside the road ahead, Will slowed the truck to a crawl. Just as he suspected, it was one of Olivia's horses. He should have mentioned to her earlier that her fence had a break in it close to the dividing line of the two properties. Did she know fences often developed breaks in the winter? Lawrence might know, but Will wasn't sure the older man was physically capable of checking to find weaknesses, much less repairing them.

Jemmy was sound asleep in his booster seat, so Will stopped, cut the engine, set the emergency brake and climbed out, then pulled a halter and lead rope from the truck bed. Every Mattson worth his or her salt knew to keep tack and tools handy in case they came across a horse running loose or some other emergency.

"Here, boy."

The sorrel gelding tossed his flaxen mane playfully and turned away.

"Aw, now, don't do that." Will dug an apple out of a grocery bag and held it out in the light reflected from his head-lights over the area. "Here you go." He held it out.

The horse tossed his head again, then gave in to the temptation and lipped the apple into his mouth. While he munched his treat and apple juice dripped to the ground, Will slipped the halter over his head and tied the lead rope to the back of the truck. He inched along the last hundred yards or so of the road to Olivia's property. Unlike the main Mattson ranch, no locked electric gate or intercom protected the entrance, so he had to climb out again to open the flimsy gate.

By the time he reached the front of the house, Jemmy had woken up. "Em'ly." He tugged against his seat belt.

"Whoa, buddy." Will unclicked the seat belt, lifted Jemmy out of the seat and carried him to the door.

After thirty seconds or so, Lawrence answered his knock. "Will, Jemmy. Welcome. Come on inside. What brings you here at this hour?"

"Dad?" Olivia appeared beside him, her dark hair tousled attractively around her face. Wow, she sure was pretty. "Will. What's going on?"

"Sorry to bug you folks, but I found your younger gelding on the road." He tilted his head back toward the truck, where the horse tugged against the lead.

Olivia gasped and charged out the door. "Dawson, what am I going to do with you?"

"Uh-oh." Lawrence clicked his tongue. "I never did get out to check the fences, even after Albert warned me that I should after the winter we had." He flicked on the outside lights, illuminating the front yard, then limped outside with the help of his cane.

They followed Olivia to the truck. All the while, Jemmy

clutched Will's shirt but watched the proceedings with wide-eyed interest.

"I can check fencing tomorrow morning," Will said. "But for now, what can we do about this rascal?"

"We?" Olivia eyed him and gave him the first real smile she'd ever cast his way in the short time since they'd met. Wow. Sure did make her even prettier. "That's very Good Samaritan of you." She untied the lead from the truck but held on to it. "We can keep him here inside the house fence."

A whinny sounded some distance away, and Dawson answered in kind.

"Sounds like his friend missed him." In the shadowed pasture some thirty yards away, Will could make out the form of the other horse.

"That's Fred." Olivia took a step in that direction. "I'd better let them say hello, or Dawson will be fussy all night."

Will and Lawrence followed her, keeping far enough behind to avoid the frisky gelding's prancing hooves.

"Horsey," Jemmy whispered.

"That's right." Will squeeze-hugged him. "Horsey. Think you'd like to ride him?"

Jemmy buried his face in Will's shoulder, but not before Will could see a tiny grin. He chuckled. He'd make a Mattson cowboy out of this little dude yet, whatever it took.

While Dawson and Fred traded over-the-fence greetings, Olive unhitched the lead and handed it to Will.

"I don't know how to thank you. I'm not worried about Fred or Buffy, our donkey, getting out. They always stick close to this side of the pasture." She brushed a hand down Dawson's neck. "Do you mind if I keep the halter on him until tomorrow?"

He shook his head. "Be my guest. And speaking of being

a guest, I'd better get over to Albert's. I have the ice cream on ice in a cooler." He nodded toward the back of the truck. "But that only keeps it from melting for so long."

"Ice ceem," Jemmy whispered in his ear.

Olivia laughed. "Ice cream at bedtime. Hmm. Well, you'd better hurry." Her friendly smile disappeared, replaced by a cross frown. "I'll close the gate after you."

Was that a dismissal? *And don't let it hit you on the way out?*

"Yeah, sure. Thanks."

"No. Thank *you*. And don't worry about the fence. I can fix it tomorrow." Her tone was definitely dismissive this time.

Will glanced at Lawrence, who shrugged and apologized with a grimace.

"Yes, ma'am. I'm sure you can do that. But since I'm looking out for Albert now, it makes sense for me to check both properties and fix anything that needs fixing."

"Whatever." She waved a hand toward his truck. "We need to get to bed."

"Yeah, sure," he repeated. "Good night."

"Good night, and thanks again." Lawrence offered a hand, and Will shook it with his free one.

As he drove around the edge of their property toward Albert's entrance, he located the break again. It wouldn't take much time to fix, so he'd try to get to it first thing tomorrow…even though Olivia was obviously indifferent to his help. He couldn't get over her odd and rapid change of mood. He knew he hadn't done anything wrong. Not so much as a dip of his eyebrows into a frown.

Wait. Had he winked at her? Maybe. It was a Mattson habit he was barely conscious of doing, but maybe she didn't know that.

One thing was sure. That feisty lady was going to fight him all the way as they planned Albert's celebration, which didn't bode well for her changing her mind about the man's promise. Which also didn't bode well for him making a safe home for Aunt Lila Rose's boys far away from the dangers of their old lives.

Somehow, whatever it took, he couldn't allow that to happen.

Olivia checked on Emily to be sure she was still asleep. Her daughter loved Dawson and would have been upset to learn he'd gotten loose. The younger gelding was too frisky for Emily now, but once she learned to ride, he would be perfect for her. For now, reliable old Fred enjoyed Emily's riding lessons as much as she did. The two horses had formed their own little herd, along with Buffy. While Fred was the alpha, no one could convince the little donkey he wasn't in charge of everything that went on in the pasture. Too bad he hadn't kept Dawson from escaping.

Olivia looked for Dad to say good-night and found him working on his model train board. The tiny N-gauge engine puffed out little bursts of smoke as it chugged around the multilevel complex of tracks through the tiny town, mountains and forest. Since Mom's death, he'd spent more and more time with the trains. When he'd showed them to Jemmy, the boy had seemed interested and for a few seconds forgot to be shy with the grown-ups. She had noticed the gratitude in Will's blue eyes.

Blue eyes? Why did she always have to think of how blue they were? Probably because of the way their color was enhanced by upper and lower eyelashes as black as his hair. Even with her own eyelashes being black, she had to add mascara to have the same effect. How annoying that a man could have such an appealing feature without working for it.

"Going to bed?" Dad interrupted her silly musings.

"Yep. I might read a few more pages of Nona's last book." She nudged his arm. "Don't you dare tell her I haven't finished it."

He chuckled. "I won't if you won't tell her I'm still working on it, too."

"Deal."

"It's a real page-turner." He used tweezers to set a tiny N-gauge person on the tiny town's sidewalk. "But these days, reading makes me sleepy."

Olivia studied his profile. He was just past sixty, but he acted like a much older man. Almost like Albert. "Maybe you should try audio books. You could listen while you work on your trains."

"Huh. Good idea." He shot her a quick grin. "That was neighborly of Will to bring Dawson home. Good of him to move in with Albert to help him out. And you got to admire him for taking care of his orphaned nephew and studying to be a foster dad so he can help his aunt with the boys she fosters." He switched off the train's power and put away his tools. "You don't meet many young men who would do all that."

Will had qualified as a foster parent? That wasn't an easy process. He must have told Dad about it while she was out of the room. Yep, he sure was a knight in shining armor. But that didn't change the threat he posed to her dreams.

"Not bad-looking, either." Dad eyed her in a teasing way.

She walked toward the door, then turned back. "Tell you what. You don't try matchmaking for me, and I won't try matchmaking for you. Deal?"

He chuckled. "No deal." His cheerful tone made him sound more like his old self than he had since Mom died. But did he really intend to keep nagging her this way?

Argh! That was all she needed. Well, he and Nona and maybe even Albert could try to push her toward Mr. Will Mattson all they wanted, but they'd never seen her dig in her heels like she was about to do. That should set them all straight. Olivia Ortiz refused to be bullied.

Yes, it was admirable that Will planned to be a foster parent. Yes, it was good of him to move in with Albert to take care of him, old family friend that he was. But as she laid her head on her pillow, another possible motive for his actions came to mind. What if he planned to use his presence in the house as a form of squatter's rights? If so, what possible counteroffensive could she launch against a man who knew the law?

Simple. She had to win the competition for the right to buy Albert's land. Then she could boot that squatter back to whatever Mattson land he probably already owned.

Chapter Four

The next day, Olivia searched online for outdoor game rentals and came up with several fun ideas. A few phone calls later, she'd reserved a bouncy house, a cornhole board with beanbags and several other games suitable for younger children. Albert had told her some of the attendees would be teens, so she brainstormed with Dad. And Nona, of course. The author would be eating supper with them every evening and, with her warm personality, already seemed like a member of the family.

"Have you ever attended a Renaissance fair?" Nona included both Dad and Olivia in her questioning. "Or Scottish Highland games?"

"Yes. We went to Scottish games in Seattle." Olivia ignored the sting of the memory and reminded herself of the fun she and Sancho had had on that last outing before his death. They'd worn red-and-green plaid kilts, and even three-year-old Emily had enjoyed the day, especially when imitating the Highland dancers.

"What competitions did they have?"

"Axe throwing, caber tossing, archery, that sort of thing. Too dangerous without professional supervision." Another memory surfaced. "They had an open competition for stone carrying called the boulder fumble. Sancho—" she managed to say his name without choking up "—just had to try it. The stone weighed about two hundred pounds, and he did pretty well running over a hundred feet before he had to drop it. The winner was this huge guy who ran over sixteen hundred feet. I was just glad Sancho didn't drop that huge stone on his foot."

She finished with a laugh. Her dear hubby had been strong, but he'd also been a good sport about not winning. Oddly, the memory of Will chopping wood, sleeves rolled up to reveal his biceps, popped into her mind. With those strong arms, he'd probably do pretty well at the boulder fumble.

Stop that! Will might be strong and undeniably handsome, but he also wanted to take away her future. Her sense of competition—and *survival*—kicked in big-time whenever she remembered that stark fact.

"That sounds like a challenge our local young men would like," Dad said. "I'm sure we can come up with more ideas. Let's keep working on it."

The brightness in his eyes brought a lump to Olivia's throat. He hadn't taken much interest in life since Mom died. If for no other reason, she needed to include him in all of her plans for Albert's birthday bash. And, of course, Nona, who was also widowed. The two of them seemed drawn to each other, but Olivia didn't know whether or not to encourage this, for lack of a better word, *friendship*. If they got too involved, what would happen to Dad when Nona finished her book and returned to her family and home responsibilities, not to mention her glamorous life as a bestselling author?

The problem was still on her mind the next day when she took Emily shopping in Riverton. Papacita's Friendly

Mart, her favorite mom-and-pop grocery, specialized in ingredients for Mexican recipes, and she hoped to get the owner's advice on how to prepare a winning sauce for her barbecue beef.

Emily had outgrown the shopping cart, so she walked beside Olivia as they wandered up and down the narrow aisles.

"Sweet pea, would you go get the milk?" At Dad's insistence, she had started letting out the leash a bit as her daughter got older, and the dairy section was just two aisles over in this small, safe store.

As always, Emily's face lit up when she was assigned an important responsibility. "Yes, ma'am." She trotted off and disappeared around the end of the soup section.

"What did I tell you?" The sound of a man's low, growling voice came from the next aisle. His question was followed by several curse words and the unmistakable sound of a hand meeting flesh. "You do as I tell you, boy, or you'll regret it. And quit yer crying, or I'll give you somethin' to cry about."

For the briefest moment, Olivia couldn't breathe or think. She'd just sent her baby in that direction. Mama-bear instincts took over, and she pushed her cart around the end of the display. Emily was nowhere in sight, but what she did see was a hulking, brown-haired man standing like an angry grizzly over a small boy of perhaps eight years.

"Now, put that under your shirt and tuck it in." He spoke in a lowered voice as he thrust a flat can of sardines at the boy.

Shaking like a leaf in the wind, Olivia swiped her phone to change the screen from her shopping list to the video camera just in time to capture the man's actions, as well as the boy's terror as he obeyed. Just as quickly, she switched back to her shopping list, then focused on the shelf beside her as though searching for a particular item. If he hurt the boy again, she would have to intervene…somehow. *Lord, please help.*

The man strode toward her. "What are you doin'?" He reached out to grab her phone.

She managed to elude his grasp and dropped the phone into her jacket pocket. "I beg your pardon?"

"Gimme that!" He grabbed her arm and reached toward the pocket.

"Let me go! How dare you?" Jerking away from him, she used her loudest, sternest voice, as Sancho had taught her to do if she was ever confronted by a bully. "Papacita!"

Papacita, no small man himself, hustled up the aisle from the meat section in the back of the store. "Senora Olivia, what…?" He took in the scene and glared at the man. "Ah, it is you. I have told you, you are no longer welcome in my store. *Vete de aquí, vete de aquí!*" He waved one muscular arm toward the door. "And do not come back."

Releasing more curses, the man grabbed the little boy's arm and strode away, deliberately knocking several items off a shelf as he went.

"Are you all right, Senora Olivia?" Papacita touched her shoulder and studied her face.

She huffed out a sigh. "Yes, thank you. But you should see this." She showed him the video. "He's not only stealing from you, but he's teaching his son to do the same. Open your phone, and I can send it to you."

As he complied, Papacita snorted. "Not his son. Him and his wife take in foster kids to make a living. I pray for those little ones. I have never seen that one, so he must be new."

"Oh, dear. I'll pray for them, too. What's his name?"

"Grant Sizemore." Papacita chuckled without humor. "Local lore says his great-grandpapa Jeb Sizemore was a cattle rustler in these parts. Seems he passed his bad ways down to that one."

"Here, Mommy." Emily shuffled carefully around the end of the aisle clutching a gallon of milk in her arms.

"Thank you, sweet pea." Olivia took the jug and placed it in the cart, then gave Papacita a significant look.

He nodded, clearly understanding there was no need to mention the drama to her daughter.

"Hi, Mr. Papacita." Emily gave him a wide grin, revealing the space in her mouth where a tooth had come out last night.

"Ah, look at you." He winked. "Now you must drink all of that milk so a new tooth will grow in."

They all laughed, which helped soften the tightness in Olivia's chest, although the memory of the incident ate at her all the way home. What if she encountered Grant Sizemore again? Riverton was a diverse, spread-out community, and she didn't recall seeing him before. Maybe she wouldn't run in to him. *Please, Lord.*

What a contrast between that man and Will Mattson. Will's tenderness toward his little nephew had impressed her from the start. That was what all kids needed. How awful to think some people took in foster children for financial gain, then taught them to steal. What kind of start did that give kids who already had too many challenges to face in life? Should she report Sizemore to the authorities? Or leave it to Papacita, who'd promised to save the video she'd given him, along with the store's CCTV?

Papacita, whose name was Ramon Martinez, had also given her a barbecue recipe and a promise to reserve some prime beef cuts when the time came. "You may depend upon it, senora—it will be the best you can buy. I only sell Mattson beef in my store."

At the time, her mind had been on the incident with the unpleasant man, but now, as she recalled Papacita's comment about his beef source, she could only roll her eyes. Mattson beef. Of course. On her way to the grocery, she'd stopped by the party-supply store to put a deposit on the bouncy house and other games, not wanting to give her credit-card number over the phone. As she'd chatted with the perky young lady at the counter, she'd noticed her name tag. Julie Mattson. *Of course.* Would there be even a single business in this town where the Mattson name didn't come up?

And would that work against her drive to win Albert's competition so she could buy his house and ensure her and Emily's future?

After Will checked the repairs in the fence breaks he'd made yesterday, with Jemmy's "help," he accepted Lawrence's invitation to see how his trains operated. He gazed around the multipurpose back room of Olivia's house. Partially filled bookshelves lined one wall, with two overstuffed chairs in front of them. At the other end of the room was a desk with a desktop computer and a table holding a printer and paper supplies. A rolling desk chair completed the picture of a functional but cozy home office.

In the center of the long room was the six-by-ten-foot train board. As promised, Lawrence had invited him to bring Jemmy over to see his N-gauge train. It was a welcome diversion and an opportunity to bring Jemmy out of himself. Aunt Lila Rose had advised a slow introduction to socialization, and this was a good step in that direction.

Despite knowing it was for the best, he was disappointed to see Olivia wasn't home. He couldn't let his natural attraction to her go any further. When Lawrence explained she was already making arrangements for Albert's birthday event, Will had a moment of annoyance. Then guilt. He was supposed to plan the food sales and baking competitions. But Aunt Lila Rose had informed him she would take charge of getting baked goods and planning the cakewalk. She would arrange the portable flooring, the music and the cakes to give away to the winners. The Old West game played at barn dances and church socials was a favorite of both Albert and Aunt Lila Rose.

Will's only task? Reserve a couple of food trucks, a job he'd completed within a half hour. Too bad Albert had decided Olivia would provide the beef, but that would have been all too easy for Will. With Olivia not knowing many people in the area, would she be able to find help as easily as he had?

He shrugged off the thought. His boys needed Albert's property, and he wasn't letting go of it without a fight. A fair fight, of course.

"Let's make this official." Lawrence put on an engineer's hat and offered a child-size one to Jemmy. "Want to wear it this time?"

Most kids loved to pop on a hat, but as he had last time, Jemmy backed against Will's legs, drawing into himself as he usually did around other people. He hadn't been afraid of Lawrence the other day, so it stung Will's heart to see his renewed shyness around the older gentleman.

Lawrence took it in stride. "Emily should be back soon, Jemmy." He set a low stool beside the train board. "When she gets here, she can join us. Until then, if you want to, you can step up and help me figure out some stuff."

Rather than pressure Jemmy, Lawrence set about his task, humming as he worked. "Now, let me see. Should this little dog be at the train station or on the playground with the little boy?" Using tweezers, he held up a tiny figure in Will's direction. "What do you think?"

"Hmm." Will caught on to his game. He struck a thoughtful pose with arms crossed and fist under his chin. "If he's at the train station, he's probably waiting for someone. If he's at the playground, he probably wants to play with the boy." He glanced at Jemmy, who was following the conversation with a solemn expression. "But boys don't want to play with dogs, do they, Jemmy?"

Jemmy's eyes widened. "I want to." It was barely a whisper, but Will's heart soared.

"Well, then." Lawrence offered the tweezers to Jemmy. "You put him where he should be."

Jemmy looked up at Will as if asking permission.

"Step right up, buddy." Will winked at him.

With his help, Jemmy stepped up on the stool and took the tweezers from Lawrence. The tiny dog fell onto the train board. Jemmy gasped and recoiled. At least he didn't run away and hide.

"Oops!" Lawrence chuckled. "Slippery little rascal, isn't he?"

Will added a soft chuckle to assure Jemmy he hadn't made a fatal mistake. It had taken him five months to assure Jemmy that he wouldn't be punished for every little slip. But in new situations, the boy often relapsed.

"Try again." Lawrence used a jolly tone. "Let's get Spot over to his pal."

This time, Jemmy held on tight and placed the figure next to the child.

"Very good." Lawrence winked at him. "Now, let's get this train moving. Want to throw the switch?"

Now fully engaged in the activity, Jemmy nodded.

The distant sound of a car door closing diverted Will's attention. Beyond the living room and through the front door, he saw Olivia and Emily taking packages from her Explorer. Olivia's thick black hair blew in the breeze, and he forced down the involuntary admiration trying to get a foothold in his chest. Manners kicked in, and he hustled out of the house.

"Hi, Emily. Olivia. Can I help?"

Olivia eyed him suspiciously, then shrugged. "Sure. Thanks."

"Say, Emily, Jemmy and your granddad are playing with the trains. How about you go see what they're up to? I'll help your mom." He'd left Jemmy without thinking and sent up a silent prayer the boy wouldn't be alarmed when he realized it.

"May I, Mom?" Emily gave Olivia a cute, questioning smile.

After a moment, she nodded. "Sure."

While Emily dashed up the walkway to the house, Olivia picked up a box of canned food, which Will hurried to grasp.

"Let me."

She hesitated, and her perfect black eyebrows arched upward, as though she was surprised by his offer. Then she released the box into his hands. It had to be pretty heavy for a petite lady like her, but she hadn't acted like it. Sure couldn't call her a wimp. Maybe this was a warning to him not to underestimate her.

"Thanks." She grabbed a bag. "I saw you fixed the fence. Much appreciated." Not looking his way or waiting for a response, she brushed past him.

It took several trips to empty the vehicle, during which time she seemed determined not to look his way. Not a problem. He didn't want her to be interested in him. Still, he couldn't resist admiring her overall attractiveness, not to mention her energy.

Leaning far into the vehicle's cargo space, she tugged at a fifty-pound bag of oats. Will moved in and picked up the bag.

"Where do you want it?"

She paused before answering, then sighed. "Over there in the shed." She waved a hand toward the small structure inside the pasture.

He made quick work of putting the bag into the shed. Although the structure had no lock, it did appear to be waterproof, which was a good thing because saddles, bridles and blankets were also stored there. He had to hand it to Olivia. She at least had the right feed and equipment to take care of the two horses and the donkey. Could she ride?

And why did he even wonder? Maybe because he hadn't been riding since Jemmy had come to live with him, and he missed it.

The final item Will lifted from the Explorer bed was a forty-pound bag of scratch-grain chicken feed.

"You have chickens?" He glanced around the yard.

"Nope. This is for Albert's flock. He provides all the eggs we can eat. He's very generous that way. The least I can do is buy him a bag of feed from time to time." She aimed a dazzling smile in the direction of Albert's yard, as if the old gentleman was standing there. "We really appreciate him."

Wow. She wasn't just pretty. When she smiled like that, she was beautiful.

Quit that! While he couldn't prevent his involuntary reactions to her beauty, her thoughtfulness and her obvious smarts, he could choose to ignore them. Best way to do that was to turn his attention to Jemmy and encourage his nephew's friendship with Emily. Besides, that smile hadn't been for him, it had been in honor of Albert's generosity toward her. Truth was, Olivia came close to turning a cold shoulder to him every time they were near each other, even when he was helping her, another reason for shutting down his attraction to her.

Who was he kidding? Olivia's lack of interest in *him* made her all the more attractive. And all the more trouble for his heart.

Olivia put away her groceries before joining the others in the train room. Emily was being a "big sister" to little Jemmy, which made Olivia proud and concerned at the same time. How would her daughter react when Jemmy and Will moved back to town, as they would have to do once Albert sold his land to her?

Why was she thinking it was a done deal? The sale was still up in the air. Will was still staying at Albert's house. And if she didn't win the right to buy the land, Jemmy—and Will—would be permanent fixtures next door, along with who knew how many rowdier boys?

Giggles coming from Jemmy and the soft paternal grin on Will's face soothed her anxiety for a moment. As she'd noted earlier, this man's care for his orphaned nephew was impressive and stood in great contrast to Grant Sizemore's cruel treatment of his little foster child. While she hadn't seen Will in other situations, she could let herself admire him for that one trait.

"Look, Jemmy. Here comes the train again." Emily pointed to the tiny engine emerging from the train-board tunnel, pulling seven cars and emitting a puff of smoke and a soft *toot-toot* to announce its arrival at the miniature train station. "Toot, toot." Emily copied the sound.

"Toot, toot," Jemmy repeated, and they both giggled.

"Mommy, may Jemmy stay for lunch?" Emily's innocent, round-eyed expression was hard to resist.

Even the boy looked her way hopefully, then stared up at Will.

"I don't know, buddy. We shouldn't invite ourselves—" Will gave Olivia a guilty shrug. "Sorry."

She looked at the bag of chicken feed, which sat propped against the wall beside the back door, waiting for Will to carry it over to Albert's place. "No need to apologize. Emily invited him." She pointed to the bag. "While you take that over to Albert, I can fix PB and J for the kids. And carrot sticks, of course."

"Of course." He chuckled. "Say, buddy." He set a hand on Jemmy's shoulder. "You don't mind staying here while I go over to Mr. Albert's, do you?"

For about two seconds, panic crossed the boy's face. Then he looked at Emily, who took his hand.

"Let's go wash our hands," she said. "We can play with my LEGOs after lunch."

That seemed to settle the matter. Jemmy carefully stepped down from the stool and let Emily lead him from the room.

Will pressed a hand to his chest as though in pain and

released a long sigh. "Wow. That little girl sure has a very special gift." He cleared his throat. "Thanks."

Her own emotions not entirely under control, Olivia barely managed a smile. "Well, you'd better take that feed over to Albert's."

He nodded and lifted the bag. "Yeah. Lawrence, thanks for showing Jemmy your train. I could tell he loved it. Did he miss me when I left the room?"

"Hmm." Dad wrinkled his forehead thoughtfully. "I think he was so fascinated by the trains that he didn't notice. Then Emily came in and they were both too interested in the operation to notice anything else."

Will glanced out the window and took a deep breath. "This has been good for him. I hope…but I don't want to intrude…"

"You bring him over anytime, Will." Dad clapped him on the shoulder. "It's no intrusion at all. I enjoy his company. And yours."

Oh, great. An open invitation to her adversary. Olivia groaned inwardly. Knowing Dad's hospitable ways, he'd probably find a way to invite all of Will's boys out from town to see the trains. If that happened, Olivia could kiss her privacy-seeking clientele goodbye.

Chapter Five

The next morning, Will made sure Chirpy was fed and locked safely in his special part of the coop before taking Jemmy outside to feed the rest of the chickens. Albert had told him the rooster could be pretty aggressive when protecting his hens, even to the point of pecking adults, so he might not hesitate to attack a little kid.

Will returned to the house and found Jemmy finishing up his blueberry and marshmallow cereal at the kitchen table, with Albert sitting across from him counting out his vitamins into daily pill organizers. Still not entirely trusting of the old man, Jemmy was okay being left in his company for a few minutes. When Will came in, the child lifted the bowl to drink the last of the purple milk, then got down from his chair and carried his bowl to the kitchen sink.

"Good job eating your breakfast." Will took the bowl and washed it. "Ready to feed those chickens?"

Jemmy nodded solemnly but said nothing. Aunt Lila Rose said it was important for him to verbalize his thoughts, something Will needed to encourage.

"What do we say?" He kept his tone light. If he spoke with even the slightest hint of disapproval, Jemmy flinched. At least he didn't cower, as he used to. But he did need to use his words, not just nod.

"Tank you?" He pointed to the newly washed bowl now sitting in the drain rack.

Will chuckled. "Sure. And you're welcome. But I meant about feeding the chickens. Want to do that with me?"

Doubt flickered across his little face, and he chewed his lip.

"Sure would appreciate you helping out, Jemmy," Albert said. He'd understood from the start how to tread lightly with the boy. "And those chickens get mighty hungry for grain after only having bugs to eat."

"Bugs!" Jemmy's face scrunched up with disgust. "Yuck."

Will and Albert chuckled, and when Jemmy saw they weren't upset with his response, he laughed, too. One of these days, Will would figure out a way to explain that chickens actually liked bugs. For now, he would just go with the flow.

"Okay, let's feed them something better." In the utility room just off the kitchen, he used his pocketknife to cut open the bag Olivia had bought. "Okay, Jemmy, this is a two-man job. I need you to take the lid off that can." He pointed to the twenty-gallon metal trash can used for feed storage.

His eyes focused and his chest puffed out with the importance of his new responsibility, Jemmy stepped right up and removed the lid, then looked at Will for approval.

"Good job." Will lifted the bag and poured the scratch grain on top of the leftover cracked corn. He'd never had the job of choosing chicken feed before and hoped Olivia had made the right choice. If not, he'd get the proper kind when he went to town. He chuckled to himself. Until then, the chickens did have their bugs.

"Okay, now let's scoop some into this bowl." Will took

a battered metal bowl from the shelf and helped Jemmy fill it. It was a bit heavy for the boy, and some slid over the side. "Oops," Will said quickly. "Don't worry. We can sweep that up later."

Once out in the sunshine, he drew in a deep breath, appreciating the freshness of the air. He'd grown up in Riverton, hardly a big city. But somehow, the air out here by the river always seemed fresher, more invigorating, much like the Mattson clan's Double Bar M Ranch a mile downriver from here. He looked forward to moving here permanently. *If* he moved here permanently.

As they approached the chicken yard, the hens made a beeline for the chicken-wire gate, clucking and climbing over each other in anticipation.

Jemmy leaned close to Will. "Do dey bite, Unka Weeoo?"

Uh-oh. He had no idea. Why had he assumed the hens wouldn't be as aggressive as the rooster?

"Tell you what. You open the gate and stand behind it, and I'll toss in a handful of feed."

Jemmy hesitated but obeyed. As he pulled the gate open, hens poured out into the yard so quickly, Will could only toss handfuls of grain in front of them. The hens scrambled to devour their share. Jemmy giggled, a sound Will had come to love.

"Here. You do it." He held out the bowl.

Jemmy scooped up a handful and tossed it, but it didn't go very far. A few hens turned their attention his way and hurried over. One of the smaller ones, pushed aside by the larger ones, looked up at Jemmy, turning her head back and forth as though looking for her share.

Against everything he'd ever done since coming to live

with Will, Jemmy handed back the bowl and picked up the little hen to let her eat from his hand. Again, he giggled.

"It tickles." But he didn't drop the food or the chicken. "Ima call her Pecky." He looked to Will for approval.

Was it a good idea to let him name the hen? If she got bigger and didn't lay eggs, she would be bound for the stew pot. He sure couldn't say that to Jemmy.

"Pecky's a fine name."

"Hey, Jemmy." Emily skipped through the flimsy gate that divided the two properties. A few steps behind her came Olivia, a wicker basket looped over her arm. "Whatcha got?"

Still holding the little hen, Jemmy ran over to his new best friend. "This is Pecky."

"Hi, Pecky." Emily petted the chicken's head as it kept eating from Jemmy's hand.

"Good morning, Jemmy." Olivia smiled that gorgeous smile at the kids—but it disappeared as she looked Will's way. "Morning."

Wow. She really didn't like him. "Hey. How's it goin'?"

"Just fine. I came over to gather eggs for Albert." She patted the basket. "But if you're doing that, we can go home."

"You don't have to go." For some self-destructive reason, he didn't want her to leave. Maybe it wasn't self-destructive. Maybe he just wanted Emily to stay for Jemmy's sake. Yeah, that was it. "We're just feeding the chickens. I'm not sure Jemmy's ready for egg gathering." He added a grin, hoping for one in return.

Nope. No smile for him.

The kids were now headed toward the chicken yard, chatting away about Jemmy's little rescue critter. "Well, I'd better get back over there and distribute the rest of this." He glanced down at the metal bowl, which was still half-full of grain, and started walking. "Then maybe you could help me herd the chickens back into their yard."

Joining him, she said, "It's better if they're outside when we gather the eggs. In fact, Albert lets them stay out most of the day. Toward evening, they always go back inside to roost." She looked toward the wooded area beyond the house. "Or if they sense danger from coyotes or snakes. Amazing creatures, these chickens."

"Huh. I didn't know that." He hadn't decided whether to keep them or not once he bought the property. How much more would he have to learn? Maybe it would be good for Jemmy and Aunt Lila Rose's boys to have the responsibility of taking care of the chickens.

"So, you didn't have chickens on your ranch?" Her almost friendly interest set off his gold-digger alarm.

"I didn't grow up on the Mattson ranch, if that's what you're referring to." He didn't intend to sound sharp. In truth, though, he was disappointed to think she was interested in his family spread, as though a man couldn't be a Mattson in these parts without being raised on the Double Bar M.

She blinked those dark brown eyes, then shrugged. "Oh." She joined the kids. "Hey, Jemmy, would you like to help us gather eggs?"

Without hesitation or a glance at Will, Jemmy nodded. Was that progress? Or danger? It was one thing for him to like playing with Emily. Another altogether for the boy to get attached to Olivia.

But Will had no way to stop it without moving back to town and forgetting his dream of owning this property and helping Aunt Lila Rose raise her foster boys. And he wasn't about to do either of those things.

* * *

"Sometimes they like to hide their eggs." Olivia moved aside a handful of straw and found a brown egg nestled near the bottom of the wooden box.

She noted that Will stood outside the wooden structure watching as they went about their chore. And no wonder. Probably an inch or two over six feet tall, he'd have to hunch over quite a bit to come in here.

She touched Jemmy's shoulder. "Want to pick it up?"

"Uh-huh." The dear little boy barely hesitated before stepping over, picking up the egg and gently placing it in Olivia's basket. He seemed to understand that eggs required careful handling.

A few feet away, Emily had already dug out two gems, one pink and the other spotted. The kids giggled, as usual, as they continued their treasure hunt. At one point, Jemmy got chicken poo on his hand. Before he could wipe it on his jeans, Olivia managed to whip out a tissue and clean him up.

"One of the hazards of the job," she said with a laugh. "After we find all the eggs, we need to clean out their boxes and put in fresh straw." She again glanced at Will, who had watched them work without comment…or one of his flashy smiles.

Although he'd been all smiles at first, something had set him off. Oh, yeah. He'd grimaced when she'd asked about chickens on his family's ranch. It seemed he hadn't grown up there—so what? She'd be sure never to mention his family again, no matter how many Mattsons she encountered in Riverton. She had no doubt they'd all be helping him win the right to buy Albert's property. If he didn't own a piece of the big ranch, maybe that was one of his reasons for wanting this bit of land. As if he couldn't find another place just as usable for his boys' ranch.

With all the eggs gathered, except an unknown number beneath one hen nesting proudly on one end of the roost, Olivia glanced at her adversary. "Could you bring over the wheelbarrow and pitchfork so we can clean out this old straw?"

He blinked those blue eyes as if surprised. "Sure." He trotted off and soon returned with a wheelbarrow full of fresh straw and the pitchfork. "Want me to do that?" Without waiting for her to answer, he hunched down and entered the small space.

A space that seemed all the smaller because of his closeness. So close that she could catch the pleasant spicy scent of his cologne.

Oh, stop it.

"I'll wait outside while you do that." Olivia scooched around his large frame and toward the door. "Come along, Emily."

They stepped out and turned to watch Will show Jemmy how to clean out the boxes and put in new straw. The pitchfork was far too big for the boy, and he still clutched the little hen under one arm, but Will let him hold on as he worked. No doubt about it, he was a good father figure. And hardworking. Again, Olivia allowed herself to respect him for those traits. Nothing more.

Yet, when she'd stood close to his very masculine presence and caught a whiff of that pleasant cologne, she had to admit it took a lot of mental wrangling to keep from admiring him. Did he know how he affected women? Did he flash that toothpaste-commercial smile just for effect? Well, he could smile all he wanted. Here was one person who wouldn't fall for it. Not when she knew that underneath it all lurked a hard heart that would steal her dreams and future security without a second thought.

"I'll take these inside." Olivia indicated her basket, which held a dozen or more eggs. After a beat, she added, "Emily, do you want to go with me or stay out here with Jemmy?"

"Stay with Jemmy." She petted the little chicken still in Jemmy's arms.

"Okay. I'll be right back." Olivia sashayed across the yard toward Albert's back door.

Will had to force his eyes back to the kids. Against his better judgment *again*, he'd enjoyed sharing chores with her. Her patience with Jemmy impressed him. Many adults ignored small kids, but she gave Jemmy as much attention as she did her own daughter.

"Say, buddy." He crouched down to eye level with Jemmy. "Don't you think Pecky would like to scratch around with the other chickens?" He waved a hand at the hens still wandering around the yard and beyond.

Shaking his head, Jemmy hugged the little hen closer. "Dey bite her."

Both kids looked up at Will with soulful eyes. He blew out a long breath.

"But you'll have to leave her outside when we go in."

Again, he hugged the hen closer. "Can she stay in my woom?"

"Uh, well…" Will scratched his chin. "That might get kinda messy. Chickens are supposed to live outside and—"

To his shock, tears welled up in Jemmy's eyes. "I pwomise she won't make a mess."

"But…"

Then it hit him. Jemmy had never stood up for himself, much less another creature. Somehow he was identifying with this scrawny little chicken and was willing to risk Will's disapproval so he could take care of her. Will had no idea how Albert would respond to it, but he couldn't stomp all over this leap in Jemmy's emotional progress.

"You promise to clean up after her, like Miss Olivia did when she cleaned your hand?"

He nodded, and a wobbly grin appeared.

"Can you use your words?"

"I pwomise."

"Okay, then. We'll have to ask Mr. Albert if it's okay, but I don't think he'll mind." The old man had told them to make themselves at home. Hopefully, that included housing a chicken in Jemmy's bedroom. Will would have to devise some sort of pen to keep Pecky from roaming—and messing—all over the house.

Emily, who'd been watching with hopeful curiosity, clapped her hands. "She can lay her eggs on your pillow."

This brought a squealy giggle from Jemmy, and both kids hopped around happily.

Will's eyes burned just a bit. Because Dad didn't allow tears, he'd never been a crier, but since his sister's death, he often found his emotions close to the surface. He shook it off with a humorless laugh under his breath. He might not have grown up on the Double Bar M Ranch, but he'd spent a good amount of his childhood there with one of his older cousins, who'd been a father figure to him. The cowboys he knew could break a leg and never shed a tear. With that example of macho behavior and Dad's disapproval, he'd never dared to cry.

"I left half of the eggs with Albert." Olivia returned with

some still in her basket. "Of course, if you plan to do any baking, I can leave these."

"Baking?" He chuckled—then noticed she was serious. "Uh, not today. And Jemmy likes cereal, so we don't eat many eggs for breakfast."

"Yes, I noticed the box of junk you feed him. Sugar, chemicals, food coloring and marshmallows. Aren't you worried about his health? His teeth?"

Oh, great. Just what Aunt Lila Rose had told him. And he still hadn't made Jemmy's first dental appointment.

Olivia wasn't finished. "You should give him yogurt. Homemade granola. Even homemade pancakes. With pure maple syrup, of course."

"Right. I'll have to think about that." Annoyance threaded up his chest. "You got any of that homemade granola we could try?"

"Of course. I'll bring some over later."

"Fine."

"Good." She motioned to Emily, who quickly obeyed. "Come along, sweet pea. You still have your lessons to finish."

To Will's surprise, the little girl made no complaint, but merely said goodbye to Jemmy and skipped after her mother with her usual happy face. What child could so cheerfully leave a playmate to do homework? Was it the difference between girls and boys? Or was Will just remiss in one more thing? Was it time to start Jemmy's schooling? His one day in preschool had been a disaster, so maybe this homeschooling thing was the way to go.

So now he had two things to ask Olivia's advice on. How to feed Jemmy and how to educate him. If he asked anyone else, other than Aunt Lila Rose, they might question his competence to raise his nephew. After five months of taking care of Jemmy, he wouldn't let himself think about losing him. In fact, he'd fight tooth and nail to be the dad the boy needed. The dad Will never had.

Chapter Six

Olivia put the roast in the oven and set the timer. "Supper's cooking, Dad. We'll be back in a half hour. Maybe a little more."

"Sounds good." Dad set his Bible on the dining table and fetched a cup of coffee. "Take your walking stick and watch for snakes."

"Oh, you don't have to tell me twice." Olivia shuddered. Somehow she had to overcome her fear of snakes so she didn't pass it on to Emily. Those slithery creatures weren't the only dangerous species making their homes by the Rio Grande.

Out in the afternoon sunshine, she and Emily stopped by the pasture shed and fed the horses their daily oats. Then they walked beyond their property and climbed the fifteen-foot-high berm that bordered the river, from where Olivia studied the fast-flowing river.

"See how high the water is? In a few weeks, when it floods, it will come up even higher."

Emily's forehead scrunched up, as it did when she had a question. "Will it come this high?"

"No." She turned and waved a hand toward Fred, Dawson and Buffy as they grazed on the spring grass. "See how level our pasture is? That was caused by the floods that came this way for many centuries. The men who built the berm years ago knew just how high to build it so our land would be protected."

Emily nodded soberly, then gave Olivia her usual sunny smile. "Grampy said he'll take me fishing."

"Sounds like fun." Olivia wouldn't mention that state officials discouraged eating fish in this part of the river. And she wasn't sure it would be safe for Emily to be so close to the river even if she learned to swim. "Let's keep walking."

They continued along the top of the berm for several minutes before descending to the bend in the road that marked the south boundary of their property. Will and Jemmy came down the road from the other direction and appeared to be exploring, too. Oddly, her heart kicked up a bit, but she dismissed her reaction as merely surprise over encountering them. After all, she hadn't seen them since they'd cleaned out the chicken coop together two days ago.

"Jemmy!" Emily ran toward her friend, and they embraced, then danced around, as they usually did.

Olivia laughed out loud. "Oh, the pure joy of children."

"So true." Will chuckled as he came closer. "And good afternoon to you, Olivia. What brings you out this fine spring day?" His blue eyes sparkled, and he gave her his usual, white-toothed smile.

Her pulse quickened as her inner defenses went on sudden alert. She looked away to focus on the kids, who were walking hand in hand toward some cardboard boxes someone had dumped near the road. "Recess from homeschooling. Emily, wait. Don't touch those boxes." She hurried toward them.

"Hold up, buddy!" Will called out. "Might be a skunk hiding in there."

Olivia snorted. "A skunk?"

He shrugged and whispered to her, "Not as scary sounding as, say, a snake?"

Even so, his warning wasn't enough to stop the children. Before Olivia and Will could reach them, they were already moving the boxes aside.

"Emily!" Olivia's heart jumped to her throat.

"Mommy, look." Emily lifted a tiny, whimpering black-and-white creature and cuddled it to her chest. "A puppy." It began to lick her face.

"Puppy!" Jemmy squealed as he pulled another one from beneath the boxes.

"Wow." Will kneeled by his nephew, who struggled to hold on to the wiggly little dog. "Look at that. What a busy little guy."

"Oh, my." Olivia crouched by Emily and instinctively petted the adorable creature. "Are there any more?"

Will moved the boxes around. "Nope. Just the two." He examined the one Jemmy held. "Somebody just dumped these little guys." Jemmy's eyes widened, and his mouth dropped open. Will paused. "I mean, maybe somebody couldn't take care of them."

"Or forgot they were in the box when they threw it away," Emily said.

Count on her daughter to find a less dismal viewpoint. Olivia took a closer look at the puppy Emily held as it tried to latch on to her finger. "Their eyes are open, but I don't think they're weaned." She turned it over. "This one's a female."

"Wonder where the mother is." Will scanned the landscape on the other side of the barbed-wire fence. "Can't see any signs of her."

"Too bad. We have so many coyotes out here. I'm glad they didn't find these little ones."

"Yeah." He leaned down to whisper in her ear. "What do you want to do?" His warm breath sent a pleasant shiver down her side.

She moved away. "Well, we sure can't leave them here."

"May I keep her?" Her daughter's soulful expression was mirrored by Jemmy's look at Will.

"Uh, um…" Olivia scrambled to think of a reason to say no. Nothing came to mind. In fact, her own heart longed to adopt this helpless creature. "At the very least," she whispered back to Will, "we have to take care of them for now."

"Unka Weeoo?" Jemmy's entire being begged the same question. "Can I keep him?"

Grimacing, Will looked at Olivia. "Got any ideas?"

"None at all. Oh, except that they have fleas." She couldn't bring herself to grab the whimpering animal from her daughter and put it back in the box. That would break Emily's heart…and her own. She'd have to find a way to get rid of the fleas later. Besides, these babies had no one else to help them.

She traded a look of resignation with Will. He nodded and gave her a half smile. In that brief moment of camaraderie, she recalled how she and Sancho had solved problems together. Two heads were definitely better than one in situations like this.

"Well, buddy." Will touched Jemmy's shoulder. "Looks like we've got some dogs to take care of. What do you think we should do first?"

"Feed them," Emily said.

"Fee' dem," Jemmy echoed.

"Well, there's that." Olivia laughed. "But I have no idea what to feed puppies."

"Tell you what." Will picked up Jemmy and his puppy. "I'll take them to my friend who's a vet. She'll have everything we need."

She? Irrational jealousy nipped at Olivia's mind. What on earth? "Sounds good."

"Let's go, then," Will said. "I'll drive. That is, if you don't mind."

"Not at all." She pulled out her cell phone and texted Dad to explain what they were doing. A few seconds later, he replied with several emojis—a dog, a grinning face, a celebratory balloon—all a clear approval of the puppy. Dad sure did love his emojis. She sent back a heart and a thumbs-up.

They walked around her property's perimeter to Albert's driveway and up to the house, where Will's truck was parked. He put Jemmy in his car seat, along with the puppy he'd chosen. Olivia hustled over to her car, which was parked behind her house, retrieved Emily's car seat and buckled her in beside Jemmy.

"Hold on to this little girl," Olivia said.

"Her name is Bitsy," Emily announced. "Jemmy, name yours Sport."

"No!" His outburst surprised them all.

"That's okay, buddy." Will patted the puppy's head. "What do you want to call him?"

"Buddy."

Will grinned. "Sounds good to me. That okay with you, Miss Emily?"

"Yes, sir." Emily was too involved with her own pup to mind the contradiction.

"So." Olivia joined Will in front, settling herself in the passenger-side bucket seat. "Bitsy and Buddy. An overload of cuteness."

Will laughed. It was a throaty baritone sound that she enjoyed a little too much. Olivia had to remind herself not to get distracted by it. Instead, as they drove along the dirt roads, she basked in the music of the kids chatting and giggling in the back seat. In some ways, she could see Jemmy was as good for her daughter as Emily was for him.

"Here comes the bump," Will called over his shoulder as they neared the final turn before reaching the highway.

Before she could brace herself, the truck bounced into and out of a dip in the dirt road, briefly jarring her.

"Bump." Will glanced in the rearview mirror.

"Bump!" Jemmy shouted, then giggled.

"Bump." Emily giggled, too.

As they sped along the highway, Olivia stared out the side window and released a quiet, melancholy sigh. This was what her life was supposed to be. Family outings, Sancho driving. Emily and Daniel safely secured in the back seat…

"Quarter for your thoughts." Will shot her his infamous smile.

She shook off her downward-spiraling mood. "A quarter? Aren't you the big spender? What happened to a penny?"

"Inflation."

Now, she laughed out loud. "Right."

Against her better judgment, she had to put aside her memories of the past and choose to enjoy this day with Emily and Jemmy. And, begrudgingly, with Will, as they took on the puppy project for their kids.

* * *

Seeing Olivia relax a bit, Will allowed himself to enjoy the moment. With the puppies diverting their attention to a common cause, maybe they could even find a way to be friends.

It hadn't taken more than a beat for him to say yes to Jemmy keeping the puppy. His nephew had found yet another needy animal to care for, something Will would encourage. It might be the key to his coming all the way out of his shell.

Will's dad had never let him have any pets, but he'd loved playing with the dogs at the Double Bar M Ranch. He had to admire Olivia for letting Emily keep the other pup. Some women he knew were too fussy to deal with animals who needed a lot of attention, like dogs. Not his female ranch cousins, of course. But his last girlfriend wouldn't even tolerate a cat. Or a child. Olivia seemed to have opened her arms and her heart to his nephew. Not to Will, of course. He could see in her eyes she didn't trust him. Considering their conflict over Albert's property, he couldn't blame her too much.

Maybe after this nonsense about who got to buy the land was over and done with, he and Olivia could be friends. He'd win, of course, and move in to be her permanent neighbor, so being friendly was important, especially out here in the boondocks, where good people looked out for one another.

He drove up the highway toward town, past adobe houses and small touristy businesses that spotted the landscape. Olivia gazed out the passenger-side window, occasionally turning her attention to the road ahead. Her profile was a work of art… *Wait.* Where on earth had that thought come from? Hadn't he decided not to think about her but to concentrate on caring for Jemmy and Aunt Lila Rose's boys? On the other hand, when a beauty like Olivia crossed his path, how could he *not* think about her?

He couldn't believe the way she'd agreed to the trip to town, had just grabbed Emily's car seat and jumped into his truck with no hesitation. Most women, even Aunt Lila Rose, demanded time to fix their hair and makeup before going out in public. Not that Olivia needed to fix anything. She even seemed unaware of her own appearance. Didn't feel the need to tuck strands of that gorgeous black hair behind her ear in a flirtatious gesture, or look his way with coy glances from beneath those long black eyelashes. Instead, her focus was on the external world, on other people and their needs. Even her business of hosting artists came from her nurturing ways.

There he went, appreciating her many fine qualities again. Somehow, he had to cram all of these thoughts in a box to be tucked away. Or dropped in the Rio Grande to flow south and out of sight.

Ha! That's not likely to happen.

He pulled into the vet's parking lot, glad to see only a few cars. Maybe they could get right in and take care of these little critters, who must be starving, if their sad little whimpers were any indication.

"I can't believe it." Olivia stared out the windshield at the sign over the front entrance. "*Mattson* Veterinary Clinic. Is there anything your family doesn't own around here?" She shot him a sarcastic look as she grasped the door handle. "I thought you said this vet is your friend."

Instead of being annoyed by her comment about his family, Will laughed. "She is a friend. She's also married to

my first cousin twice removed. Or three times. I can't remember."

Olivia rolled her eyes as she opened the door.

No, she didn't flirt with him. Or give a hoot about his
family's long lineage. And given his history with women
who flirted with him because they assumed he was rich,
that was a relief.

Sort of.

While Will saw to Jemmy and Buddy, Olivia helped
Emily from the car. Her daughter held tightly to Bitsy, who
now slept in her arms. So far, the fleas didn't seem to be
on her. Maybe they preferred to hide under Bitsy's fur. But
Emily would need a good bath before bed tonight.

Inside the clinic, Will was greeted by the receptionist, a
perky, dark-haired young woman who looked like she might
be a Mattson, too.

"Olivia, this is my cousin, June." He winked at the girl.
"Her mom, Sue, the cousin by marriage I mentioned, is
the vet, and June helps out. June, meet my neighbor, Olivia
Ortiz, and her daughter, Emily."

"Howdy, Miss Olivia, Emily. Hey there, Jemmy." June,
who appeared to be around nineteen or twenty, came around
the counter and kneeled by Emily. "What do we have here?"

"This is Bitsy." Emily returned June's smile. "That's
Buddy." She looked at Jemmy expectantly, but he moved
closer to Will.

"Well, how do you do, Bitsy." June petted the puppy.
"Would you let me take a look at this little cutie?"

Emily surrendered her new treasure. "She's hungry."

"She sure is." Letting the puppy latch on to her finger,

June laughed, then looked at Will and whispered, "No mama?"

He shook his head.

"Well, we've got just the thing." June turned to Jemmy. "Hi, Jemmy. I'm guessing Buddy's hungry, too. Will you let me give him something to eat?"

Jemmy shook his head and clutched the puppy tighter.

"No problem." June addressed both Will and Olivia. "I'll be right back."

Within minutes, she'd found bottles and milk, and had settled both kids on the waiting room couch with their puppies. "We'll get them fed before Mom checks them out." She leaned toward Olivia as though they were old friends and whispered, "And we'll get rid of those fleas."

"Tell you what." Will sat next to Jemmy. "After you feed your little buddy, we'll let June and her mom give him a checkup while we go buy him some gear."

Olivia watched the brief confusion on the boy's face. "Geuw?" As usual, he couldn't quite manage the *r*.

"Sure. He'll need toys and stuff, maybe a bed of his own."

"An' a ball."

"Definitely a ball." Will tousled Jemmy's hair.

Emily had watched the interaction with interest. She looked at Olivia. "Bitsy needs gear, too."

"Definitely."

Will winked at Olivia. And gave her that infamous smile.

Ugh! Why had she echoed his word choice? Would he take that as some sort of camaraderie?

The kids reluctantly left their new charges in June's capable hands, and soon they were on their way to the local big-box store. As they drove into the lot, Jemmy whimpered.

"Oops. I forgot." Glancing in the rearview mirror, Will whispered to Olivia, "He doesn't like this place."

As he drove out of the parking lot, Olivia bit her lip to keep from commenting. His sensitivity toward his nephew's feelings was well and good, but it could easily turn into his raising a spoiled little boy who got his way all too easily.

Then again, who was she to criticize another parent? Hadn't she let Emily keep the puppy with hardly a thought? She'd have to watch herself. Besides, Will was doing a good job with his nephew. She could respect him for that.

Now, if he would only bow out of the competition for Albert's property, she might even find herself liking the man.

Chapter Seven

~~

Will deliberately drove past the pet store owned by one of his cousins to avoid annoying Olivia...again. Instead, he chose a larger chain pet store and was glad Jemmy didn't voice any objections, maybe because he could see the dog and cat pictures painted on the window.

Inside, they found the dog department, and with a little guidance, the kids chose toys and treats. They also chose puppy-size beds, indoor kennels, collars and other supplies. Jemmy and Emily both took this task very seriously. No giggling now, just careful study of the offered merchandise and a glance or two at their respective adult before final decisions were made.

Will's heart warmed as he watched his nephew. He'd done pretty well with Pecky, and this added responsibility should further boost his self-confidence. Whether the chicken and puppy got along was a problem they'd have to solve if and when it came up.

At the checkout, he pulled out his wallet. "I'll get this." She hadn't brought a purse, and it wouldn't hurt him to spend a few bucks for Jemmy's friend.

"You don't need to do that." Olivia held up her phone. "Apple Pay." She separated Emily's stuff and shoved it toward the clerk, not giving Will a chance to object.

Not that he would. Again, she was proving herself to be different from the other women he'd known. More independent. Not expecting him to pay for everything. Certainly not clingy. He had to respect that. And if he was being honest, he'd have to admit he was relieved, too.

Back in the truck, the kids chatted about their plans for their new pets. They sounded so serious he couldn't help but smile. When their chatter became silly, Olivia coughed, apparently trying to stifle a laugh. It was the first time he'd noticed her sense of humor.

"Bitsy's gonna jump this high," Emily said.

Will could imagine her holding up a hand.

"Buddy's gonna jump dis high."

Will glanced in the rearview mirror. Yep. Jemmy's hand was higher than Emily's. Of course, his car seat was a different, higher design and gave him the advantage. And then there was the matter of training the pups *not* to jump, but they would cross that bridge when they came to it.

"Bitsy's gonna eat this much."

"Buddy's gonna eat this much."

After their giggling slowed down, Emily said, "Mommy, I'm hungry."

Will caught Olivia's eye and mouthed, *Ice cream?*

Her eyes brightened, enhancing her beauty. "Sounds good. Drive-through?"

"Right up ahead."

"Perfect."

Perfect indeed. She was turning out to be a pretty good partner in this adventure. He could see enjoying more of the same. No, he'd better shut down that thought right away.

At the order kiosk, they made their choices with little debate. When Emily asked for strawberry ice cream in a cone, Jemmy said he wanted the same. After picking up their order at the window, Will pulled into a parking spot, where he and Olivia put the provided plastic bibs on the kids before giving them their treat. Even so, Jemmy ended up with ice cream all over his face and hands. Emily managed a little better.

"Got any wet wipes?" Olivia looked around the truck cabin.

"Ugh. Meant to get some for the truck, but forgot."

She shrugged. "You got the ice cream. I'll get the wipes."

Before he could object, she trotted to the convenience store next door and returned with the needed item. The wipes did the job on the kids but left smears on his gray leather seats. He couldn't help an involuntary grimace.

"Parenting sure can be messy." Olivia gave him a sympathetic smile.

"Right." He'd known that when he signed up to care for Jemmy. But a man had a hard time releasing his pride in his truck.

Back at Sue's vet clinic, the kids got excited before they were out of the car. Both were jumping around and giggling. Will was getting used to the music of that sound.

After he introduced Olivia to his cousin Sue, they let the kids hold their puppies on the waiting-room couch, then got down to business.

"These could be purebred border collies like the ones they raise out at the ranch, but it's hard to tell at this age," Sue said. "With papers, purebreds go for about two grand apiece. Pretty expensive to be abandoned on a remote road. Did you find anything around them that might tell us where they came from?"

"Nope," Will said. "I doubt they're from the ranch. Rob

keeps tabs on everything that happens out there, and he values his dogs too much to let them go missing. And nothing in the cardboard boxes gave us a clue. Could they possibly have chips?"

"No, they're way too young." Sue blew out a breath. "You need to wait until they're eight to twelve weeks old to do that. But it looks like they have a good home. For now. Just remember, if the mother's owner comes looking for them, you may have to give them up."

"Or offer a lower price." Olivia's jaw was set just as it had been when he met her last week and she found out Will wanted to buy Albert's land. This lady didn't like to be crossed by anyone threatening her or her loved ones. While that trait might work against him, he had to respect her for it. He would do anything to protect and care for Jemmy and Aunt Lila Rose's boys.

"I don't know if that would work," he said. "Breeders need to make a profit."

"Whatever. For now, let's just get them home." Olivia walked to the couch and reached out a hand to Emily. "I just remembered I have a roast in the oven. If my dad doesn't take it out when the timer goes off, we'll be eating a brick for supper." She helped her daughter cradle Bitsy. "It was nice to meet you, Sue. June."

"Likewise," the mother and daughter chorused.

June handed Will a plastic bag with the clinic's logo on it. "This is everything you need to feed them and work on the rest of those fleas."

"Thanks. Send me the bill."

"Send half to me." Olivia smirked at Will. Ouch. She really wasn't taking anything from him.

"Say, Jemmy." June kneeled beside him. "I sure would

like to see you in my Sunday school class. We play games, have snacks and, best of all, learn all about Jesus."

Jemmy ducked his chin and moved back from her, but she kept smiling as she stood. "Emily, I'd love to see you in my class, too."

Emily returned the smile, then looked up at Olivia. "Mommy, can I go?"

Olivia sighed. "We'll see."

Sue and June followed them out to the truck, chatting with Will about family stuff. Olivia seemed to be trying not to eavesdrop, but he was glad she couldn't avoid hearing that he came from good people, that the Mattson name was respected in this town. Maybe that would motivate her to send a little respect his way, too.

Olivia settled Emily in the back seat of the truck before taking her place in the front. Beside Will. No way to avoid it. And no way to avoid the fact that he came from a nice family. June and Sue couldn't have been gentler with the puppies. Olivia would bring Bitsy back when it came time to spay her.

If someone came forward to claim the pups, well, she'd figure out how to help Emily overcome her disappointment. How would Will help Jemmy do the same? Not her problem.

But if that was so, why did she feel a pang of concern for the little boy?

"Need anything at the grocery store?" Will waved a hand toward the store coming up ahead on the right.

"No, I don't think so."

"You mind if we stop? I hate to waste a trip to town."

She shrugged. "Sure." She texted Dad to take the roast out of the oven.

He answered, Already done, and added a smiling emoji. Count on him to watch her back.

The store personnel didn't appear to object to two kids carrying puppies in the shopping carts their adults guided around the store. Olivia pushed her cart around the aisles and picked up several items she didn't need right away. But it would save her an extra trip later this week.

Once she and Emily rejoined Will and Jemmy at checkout, she couldn't ignore the sugar-laden cereals and junk food in their cart. Before she could stop herself, she snorted her disapproval.

"I suppose you have a Mattson relative who's a dentist who's going to save his teeth."

Confusion in his expression was quickly replaced by awareness. "Oh. Yeah. Well, we do get all the eggs we need from our hens, so I can make him scrambled eggs for breakfast." He grinned boyishly. "And look—I did get the orange juice with no sugar. And the no-nitrate bacon. And apples." He blinked those blue eyes, sending a jolt to her heart. "How'd I do, Mom?"

Smirking, she lifted the two boxes of cereal and a bag of chemical-flavored chips from the cart and set them on a shelf beside the checkout. "There. That's better."

"But Mom…" He reached for the chips.

Trying not to grin and failing, she smacked his hand. "No."

Now, he laughed out loud. "Yes, ma'am."

Somehow, Jemmy hadn't noticed their playful exchange, but Emily had. She grinned at both Olivia and Will. What was her daughter thinking? She really must stop this nonsense. Who in their right mind joked with the enemy, much less told them what they could or could not feed their child?

Heading home, Will drove past Albert's driveway and around to hers, then insisted on helping her take her groceries inside. Jemmy and Emily followed, puppies in hand.

"Well, what do we have here?" Dad bent down and pulled both kids into his arms. "What fine little doggies." He gently touched the pups and uttered silly words at them. Both children giggled and let him take their charges in hand.

Will stared at the scene, eyes wide, his jaw dropping.

"What?" Despite asking, Olivia understood right away. Today, Jemmy was taking to her dad without fear. "Progress," she whispered to Will.

His eyes rimmed red, he nodded. What a tender heart he had for his nephew.

And her own heart took another serious dip, like the big dip in the road to town. And just as jarring to her nerves.

"Oops." Dad stood and carried one wet puppy to the door. "They're sure not house-trained at this age. Kids, let's take them out to the porch and set down some newspapers. Then I'll get a rag to clean this up."

With Olivia and Will helping, the mess and her father were quickly cleaned up. Then Dad faced them. "So, who's going to keep them overnight?"

Just like they'd done all day, they exchanged a look, as if consulting each other came naturally.

"I assumed we'd let them stay with their new owners," Olivia said.

"Yeah." Will glanced toward the porch, where the kids now played with their furry new best friends. "We bought kennels for them to sleep in overnight."

Dad chuckled. "If you separate them, you won't be getting any sleep. They'll be howling all night missing each other. And their mama, of course."

Another shared look. If Olivia guessed correctly, her expression mirrored Will's. Eyebrows raised and jaws dropped as Dad's words sank in.

"Ho, boy." Will scrubbed a hand down his cheek, where a five-o'clock shadow had begun to appear. "Sure didn't think this through, did we?" His crooked grin sent a ping through her chest.

"Nope." She huffed out a humorless laugh that quickly morphed into a true giggle. "Any idea how to solve this?" She glanced at both men for input.

"Why not ask the children?" Nona entered the room from the back, as she'd done every afternoon since she'd arrived. Apparently, she'd heard enough of the dilemma to offer this bit of advice.

"Good idea." Dad grinned at her with a warm, familiar look that would have concerned Olivia if she didn't have a more pressing matter to deal with.

"Okay. Let's do it." Will walked to the door and called the kids in.

Emily danced into the room, cradling Bitsy in her arms. Jemmy slowly followed, clutching Buddy and looking at the adults warily. Poor little guy, so afraid of so many things. Olivia resisted the urge to sweep him up in a big hug and promise he had nothing to fear. But that would scare him more than anything. Besides, she had no right to make promises to a child who wasn't her own.

"So, kids." Will squatted down to eye level with them. "These little critters are just babies, so they need to stay together for a while longer or they might be scared and lonely. That means they'll have to stay here or over at Mr. Albert's house until they're a little older. What do you think we should do?" The tenderness in his eyes warmed Olivia's heart.

The kids looked at each other. Jemmy seemed about to cry, but Emily smiled. "Bitsy can sleep over with Jemmy and Buddy tonight. Then tomorrow night, they can stay with me."

When did her daughter become as wise as Solomon and as unselfish as The Giving Tree in the story Emily loved so much? Olivia couldn't speak for the lump in her throat.

From the soft look in his eyes, Will seemed as moved as she was.

"That's real sweet of you, Emily," he said. "Jemmy, what do you think? Can you take care of both puppies tonight and let Emily do it tomorrow night?"

Jemmy's face scrunched up, as though he was thinking it over. Then he nodded.

Will touched Jemmy's shoulder. "Use your words, buddy."

Jemmy blinked in his adorable way. "I can ta' cawe." As usual, his *r* came out as a *w*.

The relief swirling around the adults seemed almost physical, like a fresh breeze sweeping in from outdoors, uniting them all in the common cause of caring for these kids. But a nudge of concern teased at Olivia's mind. Once again, the solution had come from giving in to Jemmy's fears. Not that she thought Will should deny the boy security. But one of these days, he would have to tell him no for something or other…or end up with a child who demanded his own way all the time.

She would have to watch herself or she might be tempted to interfere, as she had in the grocery store. It was one thing to take sugary, chemical-laden cereals from Will's shopping cart—which she still couldn't believe she'd done. It was another thing entirely to intrude on his parenting. But with their lives becoming so intertwined because of the kids and their puppies, and, of course, Albert's upcoming birthday bash, how would she be able to stop herself?

"It'll be mighty fine to have dogs around again," Albert said as he helped Will and Jemmy set up the puppies' wire kennel in Jemmy's bedroom. "It's been a few years since my last one."

"Yes, sir. I know what you mean." Will was glad the old gentleman stopped before telling them whatever had happened to that last one, most likely having died of old age. Jemmy didn't need to worry about death. He'd already seen too much of that in his few years. "Dogs can bring lots of fun to our lives, can't they?"

"And companionship." Albert nudged Jemmy's shoulder. "You gonna take good care of these little rascals?"

Picking Buddy up, Jemmy nodded soberly.

Will softly cleared his throat and gave him a questioning look.

"Yes, suw," Jemmy said.

Will smiled and winked at him. After being told to shut up for most of his short life, he was learning it was okay, expected even, for him to speak up at appropriate times.

The midsize kennel had plenty of room for the dog bed and space for them to move around. After giving them their bottles—a messy operation requiring several large terry towels to absorb all the slobbered liquid—Will covered the kennel floor with a disposable absorbent mat.

"That should make cleanup a little easier." He set Bitsy inside and reached out for Buddy.

Jemmy still clutched his puppy. "I can do it." As serious as a judge, he gently set his tired little friend inside the enclosure. Looking around, he picked up Pecky, who'd been watching the whole operation with interest. "Pecky, want to go in, too?" He started to put the little chicken inside the kennel, but she squawked and jumped out of his arms. She then strutted back to her boxed perch beside Jemmy's bed in what, to Will's view, seemed like a huff. He snorted out a laugh, and Albert joined him.

"A little jealousy going on there," Albert said.

Jemmy looked from his chicken to his puppy, then up at Will, his little face scrunched with worry.

"It's okay. They'll sort it out, buddy." He'd have to find a different nickname for Jemmy now that the dog had that moniker. Pal? Short Stuff? Did he dare call him *son*? No. Not yet.

Earlier, while the kids were still playing with the pups over at Olivia's, Will had gone out to the site where they'd been abandoned to clean up the cardboard for carrying to the dump. He also searched beyond the barbed-wire fence that lined the other side of the road but found no traces of the mother. Because they were so young and not yet weaned, she must be missing them. And, if she was pure-bred, as Sue had speculated, surely somebody would be looking for her valuable offspring.

With the animals now settled, Will turned his attention to supper. Olivia had sent over a generous portion of roast beef with all the trimmings and three slices of her amazing carrot cake. Since he'd met her almost a week ago, when she'd learned about Albert's paltry food supplies, she'd checked every day to be sure the old man had at least one nourishing meal, with Will and Jemmy reaping the benefits of her cooking as well. With her natural gift for hospitality, no wonder she wanted to expand her business.

While dishing out the meal, he glanced around the dine-in kitchen and through the door into the large living room. This house was a little bigger than Olivia's place, with five bedrooms, a den and three bathrooms. Most rooms were cluttered with furniture and boxes filled with generations of memorabilia.

Yesterday, Will had found Albert sitting at his desk staring at a pile of papers, seeming unable to figure out what to do with each page. Will had offered to help him, and the old man gratefully accepted. Now, they had files for the important documents, with the rest going through the shredder. Then Albert had asked for help with the disposal of the antique furniture his grandson didn't want. Will suggested Olivia might want some of the pieces. In fact, he could envision the way she'd use these rooms for her artist clients. They'd probably love some of the solid nineteenth-century tables, cabinets and sideboards.

Why was he thinking about it from her point of view? His lawyer training, he supposed. Trying to understand a situation from both sides. But it all came down to one unchangeable point: artists and writers could live and work anywhere, while his boys needed this particular property for safety and security. Somehow, he must win the right to buy it. But could he do that without losing his, for lack of a better word, *friendship* with Olivia? Or Jemmy's all-important friendship with sweet little Emily?

In the past several days since meeting each other, the kids had formed a bond as close as he and Megan had enjoyed while growing up in their dysfunctional home. A bond that had been broken when wild, dangerous Ed came roaring up on his motorcycle and swept Megan away to what was supposed to be an exciting life. It'd been exciting, all right, but not what his naive sister had imagined.

He still didn't know how he would explain to Jemmy what a mess his parents' lives had been. Or when to do it. He'd have to do it before some busybody told the boy about the tragedy of their deaths.

He blew out a long breath. It never did any good to recall those days. If he did what scripture said and thought about things that were true and virtuous and worthy of praise, he'd have a better perspective on everything. Today's crazy and unexpected turn of events came to mind. From the discovery of the puppies, to the shopping trip, to the fun he and Jemmy had with Olivia and Emily, *those* were worthy of praise. As they'd driven back home, he'd almost felt like he had his own little family. But, of course, that could never happen, not with Olivia being so stubborn and not even liking him. She would never back down, and when he bought the property, she might not let Emily play with Jemmy. He sighed again.

Lord, only You can give us a solution that works for all of us.

With the futures of Jemmy and Aunt Lila Rose's boys on the line, he was sure God would give them this perfect place to live. Wouldn't He?

Chapter Eight

"So, it looks like you and our hero had a fun day." The glint in Nona's eyes matched the teasing grin she sent Olivia across the supper table.

"Oh, yes." Olivia refused to rise to the bait. Nona hadn't stopped teasing her about Will. "Jemmy is quite the hero for the way he—and Emily, of course—insisted on rescuing those darling little puppies."

While Dad glanced back and forth between them, Nona chuckled. "Right. Such a heroic little boy." A hint of irony colored her voice.

"Jemmy's my best friend." Emily gave Olivia a worried look. "I never had a best friend."

Uh-oh. Her daughter had begun to pick up on unspoken cues hiding in the adults' tones. "Yes, he is, sweet pea. I'm so glad you like to play with him. And I know he'll take good care of Bitsy and Buddy tonight."

Redirection usually worked, as it did now, when Emily's sweet smile returned.

"Me too." She returned to her supper, daintily picking at the broccoli she didn't care for but knew she had to eat, helped by a drizzle of melted cheese. "And tomorrow night, I get to take care of them."

"Yes, you do." Even though Olivia knew she'd do most

of the work, she found herself looking forward to this new adventure. "Nona, how's your book coming?" She'd finished reading Nona's last release yesterday evening and looked forward to the sequel.

"It's coming." She chuckled in her throaty alto way. "My characters just don't mind very well, so I'm finding the story going in a different direction."

While Olivia gaped, Dad nodded with interest and perhaps some understanding.

"What do you mean your characters don't mind very well?" Olivia said. "Don't you just write what you want them to do?"

"I wish." Nona rolled her eyes. "I always have a plan and a basic outline for my stories, but sometimes I find myself writing something entirely different because of the way my characters speak to me."

"That's the genius of creativity." Dad nodded sagely, as if he totally grasped the idea. Or maybe he wanted to impress Nona. Not that he needed to. The woman clearly liked him. A lot.

Olivia shook her head. She'd always thought writers and painters knew exactly how to ply their art. Maybe that was because she'd always planned her own life. But all her plans had been shattered by Sancho's and Daniel's deaths. And now, her business plans might be shattered as well because of the "character" who'd moved in next door.

How would her story turn out? And how could she get it back on track and write it the way she wanted to?

The next morning Emily hurried through breakfast and urged Olivia to do the same.

"Will Bitsy remember me?" she asked as they headed toward the back door.

"Once you pick her up, she'll be all over you." Olivia saw no need to discourage her by saying puppies usually liked anybody who gave them attention. They didn't become loyal companions until a little older.

Across the fence, she saw Will and Jemmy feeding the chickens, so she grabbed the egg basket by the back door. As they walked through the gate between the properties, Jemmy ran to meet them. As always, the kids gave each other a big hug, nearly falling over in their enthusiasm. And, as always, Olivia and Will laughed, both taking delight in the kids' joy. It was the only thing they agreed on.

While the kids chatted about the puppies, Will ambled over and gave Olivia one of his charming smiles, despite the weary sagging of his handsome features.

"Morning, Olivia. How are you today?"

"Better than you, it looks like." Oops. She shouldn't have been so blunt.

But to her relief, he laughed. "Yep. Those pups were pretty hungry a couple of times in the night. And, of course, they missed their mama and whimpered for quite a while."

Olivia's heart ached for the sad little pups. "And, *of course*, you didn't wake Jemmy to help."

He laughed again. "Nope. Not when he's just begun to sleep through the night without…"

"Ah." She'd been horrified when he'd told her about Jemmy's tragic first years and his recurring nightmares. "Well, it'll be our turn tonight. Dad and I already set up our kennel in Emily's room."

They watched the kids feed the chickens for a few quiet

minutes. Will's face, haggard though it appeared, had a sweet glow about it as he focused on the scene.

"I see you let Chirpy out." Olivia noticed the rooster pecking away at the grain and occasionally one of the hens.

"Yeah, he seems to accept Jemmy's not a threat, which is good." He gazed down at her, and there went that smile again. He should pose for toothpaste ads.

Somehow, her dismissive thought about his looks didn't bring the satisfaction it usually did. After yesterday, when he'd performed every task admirably regarding the abandoned puppies, she was finding it difficult to dislike him. Which didn't help her cause. Just the fact that he wanted to destroy her dream should be enough to remind her he was the enemy. Well, *destroy* might be too strong. He simply had alternate plans for the land, but it was land that should be hers.

Oh, she really had to stop this line of thinking.

"Where are the puppies?"

"Asleep in the kennel. As Sue said, they're probably just a couple weeks old, too young to bring them outside."

"Good idea." Why did his instincts have to be so spot-on? And did that mean she'd have to ask his advice as this puppy project proceeded? Since the first day they met, every situation she encountered brought them together. Against her will, she couldn't make herself dislike him, as much as she tried.

"Need anything from town?" Will broke into her musing.

She thought for a moment. "Can't think of anything. Got everything we need yesterday. Do you have to go back?"

"Yeah, I need to go by my Aunt Lila Rose's and visit with

her boys. Taking care of the puppies kept me from seeing them last evening. That's not good."

To her surprise, her eyes burned with sudden tears. How could she not respect this man who cared so much for needy boys? "I'm sure they missed you."

He shrugged and gave her a sheepish grin. "What they missed was hearing me read the next chapter of *The Fellowship of the Ring*. Since it's Saturday, I thought I'd catch them up."

"I'm sure they like you reading to them. We read to Emily, too. Right now it's *Black Beauty*. She really loves horses." She studied him for a moment. "But I'm sure those boys missed you being there, too. From what you've said, you're like a foster father to them. I'm sure you remember those fatherly bedtime hugs that gave you a sense of security."

To her surprise, he winced. "Yeah." What was that all about?

He took a step toward the kids. "Hey, Jemmy, we'd better go check on the puppies." To Olivia, he added, "Want to come?"

"Sure. Tell you what. You go ahead while Emily and I get the eggs. Then we'll come in."

"Sounds good."

As he and Jemmy walked toward the house, Olivia had to force her eyes away. If she'd ever wondered what a manly, knight-like stride might look like, Will provided the perfect example. But his reaction to her mention of a father's hug suggested he had a few chinks in his knightly armor. Instead of motivating her to hunt it down and use it to her advantage, that realization touched her heart and made her want to heal him. All against her own, and Emily's, best interests. She really must stop this sympathetic line of thinking when it came to Will Mattson. But how could she do that when they were in each other's company every day in ways she could not escape?

Will studied the tattered stolen-dog poster on the hardware store's message board and could see the markings on the purebred female looked similar to the puppies' coloring. The poster added that she answers to "Lady" and her return would garner a sizable reward. Stolen about five months ago, she could've been bred and given birth during that time. But why would the thieves dump the puppies? As much as he wanted to ignore this poster to protect Jemmy and Emily from losing their new pets, he had to do the responsible thing. He snapped a picture of the poster, then pulled off one of the phone-number tags at the bottom to call later this evening.

Jemmy looked up at him with trusting eyes. "We get 'nother puppy?" He pointed to the picture.

"No, pal. At least not yet." Will gave him a side hug. "We've got enough to do taking care of Buddy, don't you think?"

Jemmy nodded and gave him a rare full-blown grin. "Buddy's lots of work." His expression turned unsure. "Not too much."

Will tousled his hair. "No, not too much." In fact, he could see how having this responsibility, along with Pecky, had already improved Jemmy's willingness to assert himself.

When Aunt Lila Rose and her boys came out to live with them, he'd have to share Buddy, but Will would cross that bridge when he came to it. Maybe that would be the time to get another dog.

He made the purchases his aunt had requested, then drove over to her house. As usual, the boys ran out and swarmed over him with hugs, each clamoring to tell him his latest news. Today, Jemmy marched up the walk and through the front door, and even returned Aunt Lila Rose's hug.

"That's progress," she whispered as Jemmy plunked himself down in the middle of the couch rather than retreating to the corner. "I'm so pleased."

"Yeah." Will hugged her. "He's really taking this puppy thing seriously." Last evening, after Jemmy was asleep, he'd called her and related the dog saga.

She chuckled in her maternal way. "First a chicken, now a puppy. You're going to be a busy man, Will."

"Yep. Speaking of busy, before I read to the boys, I need to run by the office and sign some paperwork for Sam. Nothing to do with our boys." His cousin was also busy, but had generously taken on Will's workload along with his own. "Can I leave Jemmy with you? Sort of a trial run at encouraging his emotional independence?"

She drew in a long breath, then exhaled. "I'll try, but you be sure to keep your phone on."

"Always do."

The plan worked until Will finished his business and was on his way back to her house. When she called, he answered with his hands-free system.

"Drive safely," she said, "but Jemmy needs you, so please don't make any unnecessary stops."

"Just a few blocks away. What's happening?"

She blew out a long sigh. "Well, you know how the boys like to play a little rough. You know I grew up with three brothers, so I understand and let them have their fun. They simply meant to include Jemmy in their wrestling, but he was terrified when Jeffie tumbled him to the floor and rolled him around."

"Did he get hurt?"

"No. In fact, the other boys were having so much fun, they didn't notice Jemmy retreating to his spot in the corner of the couch."

"Crying?"

"No." Her voice hitched. "Shaking like I've never seen before. And he won't let me touch him."

"Be right there." It took all of Will's self-control to keep to the speed limit, although he did blow through an intersection on a yellow light that he would've normally stopped for.

At the house, he tried to settle his anxiety before entering by taking a deep breath. Inside the entryway, he peeked around the wall into the living room. Jemmy was huddled in the corner of the couch, eyes wide. The four other boys gradually untangled themselves and greeted him.

"We're gonna read now." Nine-year-old Benji, the undisputed leader of this little gang, grabbed the book from a side table, then plopped down on the couch.

The other three took their usual places on chairs or the floor, and Will settled in his spot between Benji and Jemmy. He started to reach out to his nephew, but Jemmy lunged toward him and snuggled under his arm, thumb in his mouth.

Will again settled his rising emotions and cleared his throat. "Hey, guys. Ready to hear the story?"

While the other boys said yes, Jemmy just stared down at the book.

"All right." Will found the page where he'd left off two nights ago. "Let's see what Frodo's up to."

After reading the chapter, he took the boys to the backyard to shoot some hoops. When he'd first started coming over to help Aunt Lila Rose, he'd lowered the hoop to a reachable height for these guys. His cousins—his aunt's three kids—had grown up in this house and always held healthy competitions on the basketball court. Still a bit too small to hold the ball, Jemmy sat on the back stoop and watched, as usual. He'd settled down during the reading and seemed okay now. As Will dribbled the ball and let his more aggressive boys snag it from him, he had an idea.

After spending a few minutes listening to each boy talk about his week, Will promised to pick them up for Sunday school in the morning. Then he and Jemmy drove to the big-box store. Although his nephew didn't like the store, once Will told him his plan, he agreed to go inside.

Purchases made, they drove back to the ranch, as he'd started to call Albert's property. This was going to be fun, and he sent up a prayer Olivia would think so, too. Once she saw what a great place it was for bringing up needy boys, maybe she'd change her mind and give up her fight to buy it.

Olivia didn't get much Saturday baking done with two little puppies to tend to. Or, to be honest with herself, two little puppies to *play* with. Dad, and even Nona, suspended all other work and hobbies to do their share of spoiling the pups. And, of course, they were the center of Emily's attention. Everyone took a turn holding their bottles, enjoying the task while it lasted. Sue had advised giving them their milk in a bowl beginning next week.

Late in the afternoon, she glanced outside and across the fence to see Will and Jemmy busy with some project. Emily saw them, too, and dashed out the back door.

"Mommy, it's basketball!" she shouted over her shoulder.

"Emily, wait."

When had her daughter become so independent? She'd never before gone outside without asking permission, but now she seemed to think Jemmy and Will were just an extension of her family. Not good, but what could Olivia do? She followed Emily and soon discovered the cause for her excitement. Will was creating a little basketball court with a plastic child-size hoop and a small ball.

"That looks like fun." She should have done this for Emily long ago. Other than their walks along the river and their occasional horse rides, they didn't get much outdoor exercise.

"Yep." Will shoveled sand into the blue plastic base of the apparatus. "My aunt's boys play basketball, so I thought Jemmy should start learning."

"Good idea." Despite her approving words, she felt a jolt. He was settling in here like he already owned the place.

"Jemmy thought we should invite Emily over to shoot some hoops. What do you think?" He winked at Emily.

"I like it." Emily danced over to Jemmy and took his hand, then frowned. "Are you okay, Jemmy?"

The caution Olivia had seen in the little boy's eyes when they first met had returned. Sympathy welled up inside her. How she would love to embrace him and promise everything would be all right, but that would only frighten him.

Emily peered in the box, picked up the reddish brown mini ball and bounced it toward Jemmy. "Catch."

A small grin appeared as he grabbed at the ball but managed to kick it instead. Both kids giggled as they clumsily chased the small basketball across the yard.

Olivia traded a look with Will. "Did something happen?" she whispered.

He nodded. "The other boys were wrestling and got a little too rough with him. They wanted to include him, but it must have thrown him back to his...former life."

Olivia frowned. "Have you tried counseling? I mean, is there anybody in Riverton who deals with childhood trauma?"

He finished with the sand and pushed the plug into the base. "I have the name of a counselor in Santa Fe. Just been putting it off. Trying to give him a sense of security here first."

Olivia couldn't imagine how she would handle the situation. When Sancho was murdered, Emily had missed him, but she'd been too young to understand why her daddy wasn't there to tuck her in at night anymore. Olivia told her Daddy was in Heaven with Jesus, and eventually, she no longer asked about him. Even with her own heart grieving, Olivia thought it best to give her daughter that sense of security Will spoke of, something every child needed and deserved. As a result, Emily's happy disposition was a joy to everyone who met her.

"Want to play?" Will tossed her a second mini ball. "Let's show them how this game is played."

Catching it, she smirked. "Game on." She bounced the ball on the hard-packed surface Will had swept clean, and took aim at the hoop, which he'd set at about four feet.

Before she could release it, he slapped it out of her hands, then swirled around and easily tossed it into the basket. He raised his arms and shouted, "Score!"

Snatching up the ball, Olivia couldn't hold in a laugh. "Emily, Jemmy. Let's gang up on this big guy."

"Hey," Will protested. "Guys against girls."

"Humph. No way." She tossed the ball in a perfect arc, landing it in the little basket.

Emily and Jemmy joined the fun and soon they were tossing the ball in wild abandon, giggling whether they made baskets or not with the two balls. They didn't even seem to notice when Olivia and Will backed off to the side to watch.

"What a great idea." Olivia looked up at Will, as always a little intimidated by his height. "When you move back to town, I'll buy it from you for Emily."

He snorted out a laugh. "Pretty sure of yourself, aren't you? I've got big plans for this place, starting with winning our Independence Day competition." He winked and gave her that white-toothed grin.

Which tickled something deep inside her. A reaction to his attractiveness? She quickly shut that down.

"You wish." She sniffed with fake annoyance. Or maybe it wasn't fake. Why had she ever agreed to their competition? This guy exuded success in everything he did, whereas she had to scramble every time she tried to inch forward. And here he was, staying on what would soon be her property. As a lawyer, he'd probably be hard to evict once she bought it.

"Hey, I saw a poster in the hardware store." He pulled his phone from his pocket and thumbed through his photos. "This is it. Could be our pups' missing mom. She was stolen."

"Oh, dear." She studied the picture of the black-and-white dog. "Could be."

"Yep, could be." He shifted his stance and started to put

his phone back in his pocket. "I'll call the number tonight after Jemmy's asleep."

Olivia watched the kids, who were bouncing around as much as the two balls they were trying to get into the hoop. "Why not call now?"

He thought for a few seconds. "Sure." He punched in the numbers. "Yeah, hi. I saw your stolen-dog poster." A pause. "Rob! Hey. Your name wasn't on the poster, and this isn't your usual number." He paused, then looked at Olivia to relay what the other person said. "Designated burner phone? Didn't want to announce that the dog belongs to a Mattson. That makes sense. Listen, we found a couple of puppies over here by Albert's place. I'm gonna text you a picture so you can see if they could be your female's pups. Get back to me, 'kay?" After hanging up, he thumbed a text into his phone and sent it.

"Let me guess. Another Mattson cousin."

"Yeah. Rob's the prime owner and manager of the Double Bar M." Will chuckled. "Everybody calls him Big Boss, which sounds pretty Old West, but it suits him. In addition to raising cattle, he raises and trains border collies for herding. This dog must be a new one because I've never seen her before."

"Little dogs herding big cattle? Wow. That must be something to see." Oops. Did that sound like a request to be invited out to the famous cattle ranch? She quickly added, "I saw border collies herding sheep at the Highland games in Seattle. Those dogs are amazing."

"Yep." He didn't seem to take offense. Maybe his guard was lowering in all matters Mattson. His phone beeped, and he opened the text. "Uh-oh. Rob thinks these pups might be Lady's."

"Uh-oh is right. The kids will be so disappointed if they have to give the pups back."

His phone beeped again. "Rob says he'll come out to see them tomorrow after church." He sighed. "Like Sue said, those dogs go for around two grand if they're purebred, so we might have to give them up. I'm not sure spending that much money is practical, at least not for me."

"Or me." Olivia's chest ached. Not only would Emily be disappointed, but she would be also. Little Bitsy and Buddy had already found a place in her heart. And she'd spent a bunch of money on the kennel and other supplies.

"Speaking of church, I've been meaning to invite you to mine." Will tucked his phone in his back pocket. "Riverton Community Church. I think you'll like Pastor Tim. He's—"

"Wait. You mean you go there, too? Why haven't I seen you?"

He stared at her for a minute. "I don't know. It's a pretty big church, and during the main service, I'm usually at the back wrangling my aunt's boys, so I can take them out if they get too fidgety. You know—come late, leave early."

"Good plan." She chuckled, glad for this change of subject. "And Dad is a front-row kind of guy, so we don't have much choice but to sit with him."

Will grunted. "Good for him. Hey, remember June invited Emily to her Sunday school class? Maybe if she went, Jemmy would feel safer there. What do you say?"

Why had she let her own insecurities keep her daughter from this important part of her spiritual education? "Sure. I'm open to any opportunity to help Jemmy. June seems like a sweet girl, and I want Emily to hear about Jesus from other people besides just Dad and me. So, yes, we'll meet you there."

His pleased grin shouldn't have made her heart flood with happiness, but it did. She was her own worst enemy. She was falling down an Alice-in-Wonderland rabbit hole and had no way to stop herself.

Chapter Nine

Will almost had himself convinced that he was spending extra time getting ready for church to honor the Lord.

It was partially true. He always shaved and combed his hair just so, even used mousse to keep that annoying cowlick curl from falling over his forehead, despite his Stetson always messing it up later. But when he chose the turquoise shirt, a turquoise-and-silver bolo tie and his new black jeans, he couldn't deny he wanted Olivia to see him at his best. In high school, Megan had always told him to wear turquoise because it made his eyes twinkle and would attract the girls.

Thoughts of his sister always brought a painful pang to his chest. She would like Olivia and—

No. He couldn't take this any further. He left on the jeans but exchanged the turquoise shirt and tie for a white shirt and black bolo, then added his plain black suit jacket before dressing Jemmy in his Sunday best shirt and a clip-on bow tie.

"Albert, are you sure you don't want to go with us?"

The old gentleman was resting in his recliner, coffee and remote in hand. "No thanks, Will. I'll just watch church here."

"You sure you can find it on Facebook?"

"Always have. Well, for as long as it's been on." He reached into his pocket and pulled out a small envelope. "Put this in the offering plate for me, will you?"

"Sure thing."

It took Will's four-door pickup and Aunt Lila Rose's van to safely transport all five boys to church. Mindful of the way one set of parents had died, Will was adamant about securing each boy in a seat belt, depending on his size. They parked next to the all-purpose building beside the one that held the sanctuary and herded four of the boys into their age-appropriate rooms. As usual, Jemmy clung to Will's hand like he'd never let go. Clutching her well-worn Bible, Aunt Lila Rose waved goodbye as she strolled toward her own class in the adult wing.

"Okay, pal, let's see if we can find cousin June." Will tried to emphasize the family connection as often as possible, hoping to give Jemmy a sense of belonging, an understanding that he had a bunch of people who loved and cared for him. Sweet June personified all of that.

He stood outside the pre-K room and peered in. Sunlight streamed in the large windows, casting a light on Olivia, who stood chatting with June. His pulse quickened, and he couldn't dismiss it as concern for Jemmy. Olivia's long black hair hung over one shoulder, and she wore a pretty yellow dress with blue flowers around the knee-length hem. Her only jewelry was a simple cross necklace and tiny pearl earrings. A hint of eye makeup she didn't usually wear brought out the sparkle of her brown eyes.

Wow. She was gorgeous.

"When you invited Emily to your class, I didn't realize you teach pre-K." Olivia glanced around the room, where a boy and two girls were playing with wooden puzzles. "Should I take Emily to another class?"

"If you think that's best." June spoke in her characteristic cheerful tone. "But I always need a helper. I'd love it if she stayed here, if just for this morning." She noticed Will standing in the door. "Hey there. Come on in." She squatted down to eye level with Jemmy. "Hi, Jemmy. Want to come in and hear some stories about Jesus?"

Not answering, he hugged closer to Will's leg and stuck his thumb in his mouth...until he saw Emily. "Em'ly." He broke away from Will and bounced over to her. The two kids hugged like they hadn't seen each other in a month instead of just yesterday.

June laughed. "Well, now I know where I stand." She looked up at Will. "He'll be fine, especially if Emily stays. Emily, do you want to stay and help me?"

"Yes, ma'am." Cute little Emily, a Mini-Me of her mother right down to the matching dress she wore, struck a maternal pose beside Jemmy.

Will chuckled, and even Olivia seemed pleased with the plan. She whispered something to her daughter and patted her on the shoulder. Emily led Jemmy to the kids' table, where they sat and began to work on a puzzle.

"Okay, you two." June smiled at Will and Olivia. "Let's get the kids registered, then off you go to find your own classes." She wrote their names and phone numbers on a form on her clipboard, then handed each of them a numbered card. "Here's your ID cards. Just tear them in half and write your child's name on one half and clip it to their tops. You keep the other half. Without that card, no one can take the kids from the room." She gave Will a significant look. Every Mattson relative knew about his custody situation and would circle the wagons if he needed their help. "Now, you two scoot. We'll be fine."

"Oh, I like this system." Olivia quickly complied, and Will followed suit.

"Just text me if you have any problems," Will said.

"Same," Olivia echoed.

They stepped out of the room into the spacious, light-filled hall. Olivia moved away from the doorway, leaned back against the wall and blew out a long breath.

"You okay?" Will also stepped beyond the doorway so Jemmy couldn't see him.

"More or less."

He chuckled. "Why? You're not worried about June?"

"Not at all. It's just that I'm not used to leaving Emily with anybody but Dad. I homeschool for a reason."

"Oh, yeah. I need to pick your brain about that. That may be the best route to go with Jemmy."

She stared up at him, and his pulse picked up again. Those brown eyes...

"I can pass Emily's kindergarten materials on to you. We homeschoolers do that a lot. That way you can see if it's right for Jemmy before you spend any money."

"I'd like that." With some difficulty, he broke eye contact and looked down the hall toward the lobby. "So, you haven't found a Sunday-school class yet?" Stupid question. If she had, she'd have already enrolled Emily in one for her own age.

"No." She chewed her lip. "Guess I'm as shy as Jemmy about trying new situations."

A familiar protective feeling stirred in his chest—a feeling often directed toward Jemmy, Aunt Lila Rose and her kids. A feeling he'd once directed toward Megan. But nothing he felt or did had kept his sister safe.

He shoved away the dismal memory and focused on the present…and Olivia. When had he begun to include this usually feisty woman in his circle of responsibility?

"If you want to, we can sit down there in the lobby." Will waved in that direction.

"You don't want to go to your class?"

He shrugged. "Ever since Jemmy's needed me twenty-four-seven, I've sort of gotten out of the Sunday school habit." That sounded pretty pathetic. He should go today and take Olivia with him. Instead, he informed her, "I'll just wait down there so I'll be close if he needs me." He chuckled. "Or, more accurately, if June needs me."

"Sounds like a plan." Olivia started walking toward the lobby. "Mind if I join you?"

"Not at all." No, he didn't mind in the least. Against everything that made sense in his life, he wanted to spend more time with this kind, beautiful woman who just happened to threaten the destruction of his dearest dream… and had maybe even wiggled her way into his heart without the slightest effort.

"We usually go out for lunch on Sundays," Dad said to Will on the front lawn of the church. "Can we tempt you to join us?" With Nona beside him, he seemed happier than Olivia had seen him since Mom had died.

As for his invitation to Will and company, she was less than pleased. Somehow, she'd found herself seated next to Will during the service. Even though he kept busy making sure his boys behaved, he managed to send her an occasional smile. After the first time, when her heart did a silly little flip-flop, she forced her attention back to the sermon.

Before Will could answer Dad, she piped up. "We should get back to the puppies. They're probably starving. We've been gone three hours."

"Oh. Right." Dad gave her a sheepish grin. "Well, this is why we drive separately. I'm taking Nona to lunch, and I'll see you all at home." He nodded to Will's aunt. "Nice to meet you, Mrs. Jenson."

"Nice to meet you, too, Lawrence. And Nona. Please, everybody calls me Lila Rose."

"Then that's what we'll do, ma'am." He seemed to include Nona in that *we*. "You all have a nice lunch."

As Dad and Nona walked away, Will and his aunt corralled their charges, who'd been chasing each other around on the grass.

"These boys are hungry as bears," Mrs. Jensen said. "We'd better do drive-through, Will."

"Yes, ma'am." He gave Olivia an apologetic grimace, then smiled. "Tell you what. Since you're taking care of Buddy for us, I'll bring you some of that drive-through as soon as the boys are settled."

"Please say yes, Mommy." Emily gave her a hopeful smile.

Olivia brushed a hand over Emily's cheek. "Honey, that's a long time to wait for lunch. Aren't you already hungry? I am." She turned to Will. "Thanks, but we'll do our own drive-through."

"Can Jemmy come with us?" Emily reached out to the boy, who was hugging close to Will. "Jemmy, want to come with us?"

"Oh, I'm not sure—" Will stopped, probably because Jemmy had already taken Emily's hand. And he was smiling.

"I—I don't know." Doubt, and maybe a hint of fear, crossed Will's face. Then decision. He squatted down to Jemmy's level. "Say, pal, would you be okay going with Emily and Miss Olivia while I take your brothers home?"

Jemmy's eyes widened briefly. Then he nodded. "I want to go with Em'ly."

Will looked up at Olivia. "Is that okay with you?"

She'd been so taken up with the emotion of the moment, she hadn't considered what this meant. Would this darling little boy trust her? Or would he suddenly realize Will wasn't with them and become frightened? If that happened, how would she manage it? The kids smiled up at her, trust shining in their eyes and sealing her decision.

"I'll need his car seat."

"Right." Will jogged over to his truck and soon had the seat buckled into her Explorer.

"Come on, Jemmy." Emily climbed into her spot and secured herself in her car seat.

Without hesitation, he followed her and let Will buckle him in.

"Bye, pal. See you soon." Will tousled Jemmy's hair.

For one brief moment, doubt crossed the boy's face. Then he said, "Bye, pal. See you soon."

His eyes suspiciously moist, Will backed up and closed the door. "I'd better get going and help my aunt with her boys."

"Okay." Olivia hopped in the car and made her escape before her emotions took over. With the drive home taking twenty minutes and the long line they'd surely find at the drive-through, she worried about the puppies. "Let's get home and take care of those puppies. You two okay with PB and J?"

"Puppies and PB and J!" Emily squealed.

"Puppies and PB and J!" Jemmy echoed.

Then they both giggled with abandon and started one of their adorably silly conversations about their new pets.

Olivia had to blink hard to clear the tears from her eyes. This dear little boy had made amazing progress in the short week and a day she and Emily had known him. And all due to her daughter's gentle, loving ways. While Emily didn't understand what was at stake, Olivia couldn't think of denying either child their friendship.

Lord, help. I don't know how to keep from losing my right to buy Albert's property. Please don't let that happen. Please show me what to do.

This morning, Pastor Tim had expounded on Proverbs 3:5-6 in his sermon. But how could she "lean not on" her own understanding of the situation and choose to "trust in the Lord with all" her heart when her and her daughter's future depended on owning Albert's land? Hadn't He already directed her "path" to have this dream in the first place?

She couldn't solve her problems today, so she set aside her worries and started singing "Jesus Loves Me," as she and Emily often did while out for a drive. The kids joined in with their sweet voices, which lifted her mood, at least for the moment.

They arrived home to find the puppies yipping and whining.

"Looks like we need to feed them first." Olivia settled each child on the floor with a puppy and a bottle while she cleaned up the kennel. Much giggling and silly chatter ensued, making music for her heart and further improving her day. If not for her fears about the future, she could enjoy the sweetness of these moments with the same carefree abandon as the kids.

* * *

Will parked at Albert's and took in the hamburger and fries he'd bought for the old man. "Did you eat yet?"

"No. Wasn't in the mood. That hamburger smells mighty good, though." He sat at the kitchen table and opened the bag. "Join me?"

"Thanks, but I need to check on Jemmy." Give or take a few brief times, they'd been constant companions for the past five months, so it felt strange not to have Jemmy with him.

He hustled across the two yards and knocked on Olivia's back door. When she opened it to greet him, he felt a kick under his ribs. Wow, she looked cute. She'd changed out of her church dress and into jeans and an orange T-shirt, which she'd tied at the waist. Her hair was a bit mussed, and she smelled like peanut butter. For a moment, he couldn't speak.

"Hey." She blinked those dark brown eyes. "Come on in."

He did. "Sorry it took so long for me to get back. My aunt's boys needed some attention after lunch." He glanced beyond her. "How's Jemmy?"

"Fine." She smiled, and another kick hit him under the ribs.

"No problems?" Relief flooded his chest.

She laughed, that musical sound he'd like to hear more often. "Not a one. You give a kid a puppy and PB and J, and all is bliss."

He chuckled. "True that." He stared down at her, wishing he could dismiss this knot of reserve he felt toward her. "Well, I'd better check on him."

"Sure. He's napping in Emily's bed. With Buddy, of course."

"Napping? Yeah, I guess he's exhausted from his busy day."

They walked toward Emily's room and, sure enough, Jemmy was sound asleep, with one arm around his sleeping Buddy.

Will exhaled a long sigh. "Man, that's a beautiful sight," he whispered. "He looks like he doesn't have a care in the world."

"I know. Isn't that sweet?" she whispered back.

The maternal look in her eyes further stirred Will's emotions. Her genuine affection for a child not her own was truly incredible.

"Mommy, is Jemmy awake yet?" Emily bounced into the room with Bitsy tucked under one arm. "We want to take the puppies outside to play."

Her cheerful and not-so-quiet voice woke Jemmy, and he sat up in alarm. Eyes wide, he seemed to survey his surroundings before settling his stare. "Unka Weeoo." He scrambled from the bed, leaving Buddy behind, and headed toward Will. Then he stopped and turned around to retrieve his whimpering puppy.

"Come on, Jemmy. Let's go outside." Emily nudged him. "Mommy, we can go outside, can't we?"

Olivia looked up at Will, something he'd begun to like... a lot. "What do you think?"

"Can't hurt."

They trooped outdoors to the south side of the house, where the kids sat on the grass near the budding peach and apple trees to let their pets explore their surroundings. Not yet fully standing on their chubby little legs, the fuzz balls lumbered around, sniffing the grass, falling over and wrestling with each other. They also nipped at each other's ears, resulting in yips of complaint. Every movement was met with squeals and giggles from the kids.

As he watched, Will had an idea.

"Hey, Jemmy." He settled on the grass beside his nephew. "See how Bitsy and Buddy wrestle around with each other?"

Jemmy looked up at him, trust beaming from his eyes. "Yes, suw."

"That's what puppies do. And little boys, too. Like your brothers." Following Aunt Lila Rose's suggestion, he'd started calling all the boys "brothers" to give them a sense of family.

Jemmy stared down. "I don't like to w'estle. It huwts."

"They don't mean to hurt you, just like Buddy doesn't mean to hurt Bitsy."

The male puppy chose that moment to nip his sister, and she yipped in complaint. Will winced as he exchanged a look with Olivia. She shrugged and shook her head.

"No, Buddy." Jemmy snatched up his puppy. "Don't huwt her."

"It's okay." Emily picked up Bitsy. "She's okay. Like when we played basketball and you bumped me and I fell down. It didn't hurt."

Jemmy frowned and seemed to digest that idea. The puppies caught his attention again, and he jumped to his feet. "Come on, Buddy. Follow me."

Buddy wandered in a different direction, clearly not getting the message.

"Well, I'd better put supper in the slow cooker." Olivia reached for Emily's hand. "Let's go, sweet pea."

Will didn't want their time together to end. "Can I help? I'm a pretty good sous chef."

She side-eyed him and gave him a mischievous grin. "Are you inviting yourself to supper?"

Heat raced up his neck. "Didn't mean to. I just—" What

excuse could he give? "Just wanted to let Jemmy play with Emily a little longer, if that's okay with you."

"Right." She laughed in her musical way. "Sure. Tell you what. You can help me show the puppies how to drink from a dish. That's next on the timeline Sue gave us."

"Hey, Will." Cousin Rob strode across the yard from Albert's place. "Are those the pups?"

"Hey, cuz." As Rob reached them, Will had to settle his heart. If he took the puppies, it would devastate Jemmy. "Yep. And this is my neighbor, Olivia Ortiz, and her daughter, Emily. You know Jemmy, of course. Olivia, this is Robert Allen Mattson the Fifth, owner of the Double Bar M Ranch, and otherwise known as Big Boss."

Rob shorted. "Some call me that. You can call me Rob." He grinned and touched the brim of his Stetson. "Nice to meet you, ma'am."

"I'm glad to meet you, Rob." Despite her polite words, she gave him a wary look.

"Don't mean to be rude, but I gotta get back to the ranch. You mind if I look over the pups?"

Will traded a look with Olivia, something that was becoming all too natural.

"Sure." She walked over to Emily. "Sweet pea, do you mind if I show Bitsy to Mr. Rob?"

Trust shining in her eyes, Emily smiled as she handed the puppy to her mother. Jemmy clutched Buddy and stared up at Will, fear written all over his face. Will tried to give him an encouraging smile, but it felt more like a grimace.

Rob gently took Bitsy in hand and examined her markings, then scratched behind her ears. "Sure does look like one of ours. And very much like the pups sired by our main breeding male. We bought Lady to introduce new blood to our kennel and to teach my kids some responsibility. Sadly, she went missing after just a few days." He glanced at Jemmy and sighed. "If Lady was pregnant when she was stolen, these are undoubtedly hers. The timing's just about right."

Olivia's shoulders slumped. "That's what I was afraid of."

The children's eyes were now wide and focused on the adults.

They all watched as Jemmy took a step toward the house, Buddy held tightly in his arms.

Rob let out a long sigh. "Tell you what. Let's do DNA testing to find out their parentage. We keep the DNA on all our animals, especially those with papers."

"Wow. You can do that? It sure would be helpful." Olivia kneeled down beside Emily. "Mr. Rob's going to take Bitsy for a little while…"

"Oh, no, ma'am." Rob handed Bitsy back to Emily, kneeled down, then reached into his jacket pocket and brought out two small boxes. "We can do it here and now. Just won't get the results back for a while." He'd already labeled the boxes *male* and *female* with a Sharpie.

"Blood samples?" Will could imagine the complaints the pups would make if they had to be poked with needles. And the kids would probably get upset, too.

Rob shook his head. "Cheek swabs. Now, Emily, can you hold Bitsy for me?"

"Yes, sir." Her adorable, trusting smile brought a lump to Will's throat.

Rob tore open the box labeled *female* and pulled out a swab, making a big show of his actions. "Now, Bitsy, open wide." He held Bitsy's lower jaw and swabbed for several seconds before putting the swab into a small vial. "Good girl. That should do it. Thank you, Miss Emily." He ruffled the pup's head. "Okay, Jemmy, how about your little fella?" He motioned to him.

Eyes filling with tears, Jemmy walked slowly toward Will and offered his beloved pet to Rob.

"You can hold him," Will urged. "Come on now. Let Cousin Rob tickle his mouth."

Rob kneeled down again to repeat the procedure, only to have Buddy bite the swab in two and try to eat it. "Uh-oh." While everyone else laughed, Rob gripped Buddy's lower jaw and managed to extract the cotton-covered stick. "Whew. That was close. Wouldn't do for him to swallow it. Thank you, Jemmy."

Jemmy eyed him with a hint of confusion. Like most of the Mattson men in the area, Rob and Will resembled each other. Even with their age difference of around twelve years, maybe Jemmy could see he was family.

"So, do you want some help loading them into your truck?" Will tilted his head toward Albert's place, where Rob's truck was parked.

"Naw. You keep them for now." Rob ruffled Buddy's head. "Jemmy, you sure are taking good care of these little critters. Look how fat and furry they are. Keep up the good work."

Jemmy gave him a tiny smile, and his tears vanished. Progress!

"Okay, then." Rob stood. "I'll let you know as soon as I get the DNA results in maybe ten days, two weeks. Could be longer if the lab is busy." He tipped his hat to Olivia. "Nice to meet you, ma'am. The whole Mattson clan's been praying for this chump to find the right lady, and here you're right next door—"

"Whoa!" Will couldn't let him continue. "Let's not go there."

"Not hardly." Olivia glared at Rob. "The only things Will and I agree on are our kids and their puppies. If you want to pray for anything for Emily and me, pray that DNA won't match your dogs."

Rob gave her a sympathetic nod. "Yes, ma'am." He touched his hat brim again, then strode away.

"Sorry." Will gave her a sheepish grin. "Don't take him too seriously. As he said, the entire clan's been trying to marry me off for years."

She rolled her eyes and walked away toward the children.

This whole conversation made Will's heart sink. She obviously didn't like him, but he was afraid he was falling for her.

No. Couldn't be. As she said, the only things they had in common were the kids and their pups. With their dispute over who would win the right to buy Albert's property, that was hardly enough to build a relationship on. How could he continue to spend so much time with her and Emily for Jemmy's sake and yet protect his own heart at the same time?

Simple answer. He couldn't.

Chapter Ten

~

In the small, three-stall horse shed, Olivia helped Emily give Fred a good brushing, removing the last of his winter coat.

"Okay, now the blanket." She watched Emily lift the woven saddle blanket from its hanger and try to toss it over Fred's fifteen hands height, maybe twenty inches above her three and a half feet. It slid to the ground on his other side, and they both laughed.

"Oops." Emily scurried around him, picked it up and tried again.

This time, Olivia settled it in place. "There. Now, my turn." She hefted the child-size saddle, tossed it over Fred's back and secured the cinch.

While she double-checked the halter and reins, Emily moved to Fred's head and chatted to him. The old gelding nuzzled her and leaned into her caresses, soaking up and returning her affection.

Impossibly cute in her jeans, T-shirt and Western boots, Emily had all the promise of a little rodeo queen. Not that Olivia had such ambitions for her daughter, but Emily always loved to see the queens at the rodeos they attended. If she showed an interest in competing, that might be the Lord's way of directing her path.

She led Fred out into the morning sunshine and breathed

in the fresh country air. She loved this place. Loved that her grandparents had left such a beautiful legacy for the family. Why did Will have to go and ruin everything by wanting to clutter this peaceful place with rambunctious boys? On Sunday, his aunt's four foster sons had chased each other around the churchyard like a pack of playful puppies…although she had to admit they obeyed Lila Rose and Will without too much objection when it was time to go home. Maybe it was the promise of drive-through hamburgers that settled them down.

"Up you go." She lifted Emily into the saddle and adjusted the stirrups to the right length. "You remember your knee signals?"

"Yes, ma'am. Can I take the reins?" She giggled. "*May* I take the reins?"

"Maybe in a bit. Let's be sure you have your balance." She led Fred around the perimeter of the grassy pasture. The dear old horse plodded along at an even pace, seemingly mindful of his precious load. When Olivia trotted for a few yards, Fred kept pace and slowed when she did.

As they came back around toward the shed, where Dawson and Buffy watched them with mild interest, Emily waved furiously and called out, "Jemmy! Come ride with me!"

Looking in that direction, Olivia felt her heart skip. Sure enough, there were Will and Jemmy, looking for all the world like genuine cowboys. Light blue jeans, matching blue plaid, open-collar shirts, Western boots and brown Stetson hats. Jemmy looked adorable. Will looked like a cowgirl's dream come true.

Ugh! Why couldn't she keep such thoughts at bay? She

constantly needed to remind herself his looks were a charming facade that hid his plans to steal her livelihood.

"Since you didn't come over to collect eggs this morning, I brought you some." Will held up a small bowl. "I see you're busy. Want me to take them inside?"

"Thanks, but no. Just put them over there by the shed." She nodded in that direction, and he complied.

"Jemmy, want to ride with me?" Emily repeated her invitation. "You can sit in front of me."

He stared up at her, fear and indecision in his eyes. An ache that was becoming very familiar regarding this little boy surged up in Olivia's chest. What could she do to reassure him?

"What do you say, pal?" Will asked as he returned. "Want to ride?" He looked at Olivia. "You mind?"

"Not at all." Olivia bent down to Jemmy. "See how gentle Fred is? He loves little boys and girls. And Uncle Will can walk beside you while you ride."

Will shot her a warm look she felt clear down to her toes. Against everything that made sense in her life, she wouldn't trade this desire to help Jemmy for anything. Her involuntary reactions to his uncle were another matter entirely.

Finally convinced, Jemmy lifted his arms to Will, who gently set him up in front of Emily.

"'S'too high," Jemmy whined as he reached for Will.

"Aw, come on, Jemmy. It's fun." Emily pulled him back with a hug, causing his hat to slip down over his nose. "I won't let you fall."

He lifted the hat, indecision in his eyes, but said, "Okay."

As they walked around the pasture, Olivia on one side of Fred and Will on the other, she once again had that sense of family. Maybe Will and Jemmy weren't Sancho and Daniel, but they weren't bad substitutes. *The Lord giveth and the Lord taketh away. Blessed be the Name of the Lord.* Was it possible God was giving her and Emily a family for the one they'd lost?

What a wild, not to mention inconvenient, thought. Will came with too much baggage. Not just his vast Mattson clan, but his aunt's posse of little boys that he wanted to let loose on her quiet corner of the world. And Will intended to bring other boys out here as well. She couldn't be a part of that life. What about her plans? Her dreams? She wasn't ready to lose her independence and her very means of supporting herself and Emily.

Besides, she couldn't trust Will's charming ways. He was all cowboy manners and nice words, but she didn't doubt that was all part of his plan to win the competition she'd been so foolish to enter with him.

They came back around to the shed, and she reached up for Jemmy. "How did you like riding?"

"I like it." He gave her an adorable smile and fell into her arms.

Without thinking, she hugged him close, savoring the sweetness of his returned embrace. "I'm so glad." She set him down and turned to help Emily, only to see Will had claimed the honor.

Emily giggled and hugged his neck. "Thank you, Mr. Will."

"You're welcome, Miss Emily." He held her for a few seconds, his eyes suspiciously moist, then let her down. "We'll have to do this again, won't we?"

The emotion written on his face was real. His gentleness with Emily was real. And he was a good father to Jemmy.

Despite everything she feared about him, she felt her list of objections begin to fade.

"Jemmy, want to play?" Emily took his hand. "Mommy and I are gonna stuff bags."

"Yay!" Jemmy bounced up and down. "Stuff bags."

"Stuff bags?" Will laughed. "Sure sounds like all kinds of fun." The smirk on his face contradicted his words.

"Humph." Olivia sniffed and lifted her chin with mock superiority. "Obviously, you've never filled grab bags. It can be very gratifying to put party treats in a red, white and blue bag."

"Ah. Now I see the method for your madness." Will copied her expression. "Am I right in guessing this is all about enticing people to vote for you on Independence Day?"

She blinked, attempting to look innocent. "Why, Mr. Mattson, are you accusing me of trying to sway the judges?"

"Not just accusing." Will crossed his arms and stared down his nose at her. "Indicting, deliberating and finding you guilty."

"Uh-oh. Lawyer speak." Olivia shuddered comically. "Now I'm really scared."

He chuckled. "You should be. I have a few secret weapons of my own."

"Such as?"

"You'll have to wait and see like everybody else."

Secret weapons. That was exactly what she was afraid of. He planned to pull some rabbits out of that Stetson hat, while she was still sliding down Alice's rabbit hole into a wonderland she wanted no part of.

Will tried to convince himself he was helping the enemy, but Jemmy was having too much fun for Will to think of

Olivia in that way. They set up fifty or sixty flag-covered paper bags on her dining-room table to be filled with candy, small toys, puzzles, toothbrushes, travel-size toothpaste, combs, socks, crayons and coloring books that were all lying in shoeboxes on the sideboard.

"This is really cool stuff," Will said. "Just what the children in this area would appreciate. Where'd you get the idea?"

"I can't take credit for it." Olivia opened a bag of individually wrapped lollypops and poured them into a bowl. "Dad and Nona went to the party store and loaded up on all of this."

"Ah. You have helpers. Guess I'm gonna have to step up my game."

She shot him a withering look. "I'm sure you have plenty of people to help you."

Will shrugged. "Maybe so. Maybe not."

Her attempt at a rebutting snort ended on a chuckle.

He loved watching her laugh, even at his own expense. Loved their bantering. Loved spending time with her. She was quite a woman. And although she didn't want Aunt Lila Rose's boys to live next door, she couldn't hide her affection for kids—even ones who weren't her own, especially Jemmy.

Today, Jemmy didn't seem to have a care in the world. He'd had fun riding the horse and now followed Olivia and Emily around the table, reaching up on tiptoes to put the various items into the bags. As usual, he was as serious as a judge with this responsibility.

Thinking of judges reminded Will of his July appointment with Judge Mathis, who would have the final say about his adoption application. Will's Mattson name notwithstanding, a single man of twenty-eight who lived in an apartment might be seen by some people as a less-than-ideal adoptive father, even with Aunt Lila Rose supporting him. If Grant Sizemore had his way, he and Mabel would gain custody because Mabel was Ed's sister. If their application was favored over Will's, Jemmy's life would take a seriously bad turn. It didn't take much to figure out Grant and Mabel fostered children for the money, but if Will tried to prove it, they might accuse him of slander intended to undercut their own claims. Surely Judge Mathis would be able to discern what rotten foster parents they were.

Maybe Will had made a mistake to take this route. Maybe he should have bought a house in town, but he'd been saving up for a long time to buy Albert's place outright. He couldn't afford to buy both properties. Maybe he should have asked Aunt Lila Rose to apply to be Jemmy's foster mom, but Jemmy still needed to learn how to trust the other boys before he'd feel safe living with them. No, the only solution was for Will to buy Albert's land and prove himself a responsible parent.

"Are you sure you kids aren't tired of PB and J?" Olivia had begun fixing lunch as though it was their everyday routine. "We could make tacos."

"PB and J," Emily and Jemmy chorused.

"How about you?" Olivia glanced at Will. "I can make those tacos for us."

"That's okay. PB and J works for me." How could it seem so natural to watch her prepping lunch for everyone? Just like he imagined a real family, something he'd never really experienced. "As long as we have carrot sticks."

She side-eyed him. "What? No chips? Sounds like I'm converting you to healthy eating."

He snorted out a laugh. "Could be." He wouldn't argue with her, not after the way she'd held on to Jemmy after she took him off the horse. She honestly cared about his nephew. Of course, he'd fallen in love with sweet little Emily, who was changing Jemmy's life more than anyone since his parents' deaths had traumatized him. How could Will not love her? And maybe, just maybe—although he'd known them less than two weeks—he was falling for Emily's mother, too.

That thought wouldn't leave him for the rest of the day and even stuck in his brain when he and Jemmy drove to Aunt Lila Rose's house. After greeting the boys, reading a chapter to them and tucking each one into bed with individual prayers, he settled a sleeping Jemmy on the couch and joined his aunt for coffee in the kitchen.

"You're falling for her, aren't you?" Aunt Lila Rose peered at him over her steaming cup, mischief in her blue eyes.

"Falling for who?" Will lowered his eyes, avoiding her intense gaze.

"Darlin', I've known you since before you were born. I can tell when you're avoiding the obvious. When you and Olivia came walking across the churchyard on Sunday, the way you looked at her gave you away."

"Aw, come on. I barely know her." He needed to figure this out for himself without his aunt's two cents.

She chuckled. "It's not quantity of time, it's quality. Besides, you said you're over at her place almost every day. I'm beginning to wonder if you're actually taking care of Albert."

"As much as he'll let me." Will grunted. "At least I persuaded him to sign over power of attorney to his grandson. That way, if he...well, you know."

"Yes." She gave him a sad smile. "Joe Winslow's a fine man. I know he'll do what's right by Albert when the time comes." She leaned toward him. "And don't change the subject. What are you going to do about your relationship with Olivia?"

"It's not a relationship. It's…" He couldn't find the right word, which caused a stupid little ache in his chest. What on earth?

"Okay, then. I won't say any more." Her eyes took on a mischievous glint. "Tonight. No promises about tomorrow."

He shook his head. When Aunt Lila Rose latched on to an idea, she didn't let go.

He set a hand on hers. "Please keep praying that we can buy Albert's property. The more time I spend out there, the more I know it's the right place for you and your boys and Jemmy. I didn't want to get the boys' hopes up, so I didn't mention this to them, but this morning Jemmy got to ride Olivia's horse with Emily."

"Oh, how wonderful." Aunt Lila Rose beamed. "I haven't ridden for several years, but growing up on the ranch, it was my favorite pastime. It'll be fun to introduce the boys to horses." She wrinkled her forehead into a thoughtful expression. "I should probably talk to a realtor about selling this place."

Will released a long sigh. "Better hold off on that. Buying Albert's place isn't a done deal."

"Maybe not, but we'll give that competition our best shot." She grinned. "Wait 'til you see the cakes and cookies I plan to bring. We'll wow the attendees and ensure their votes."

Will cringed inwardly. To hear his aunt talk, this would be nothing more than a local fair where everybody had a good time amid friendly competition. But for him, as well as for all the boys he longed to bring up in safety and security, it was the making or breaking of a dream. He had to win. *Had* to.

But if, against his better judgment, he was starting to care for Olivia, how could he squash her dreams without destroying any chance he might have of developing a meaningful and possibly permanent relationship with her?

Simple answer: he couldn't.

The last time Olivia wandered through a monument-supply business, it had been to choose Sancho's headstone. This time she didn't search through tears, but with a clear-eyed gaze as she chose uncut stones for her boulder fumble. While memories of Sancho still had the power to stir her emotions, today she was laser-focused on survival for herself and Emily.

The manager had directed her to the yard's back section, where rejected rocks of varying shapes and sizes had been laid out in orderly rows. Olivia decided on one that looked the right size for men and older boys to carry and a smaller one for any women who might want to join the fun. At the Highland games she'd attended, a whole team of female athletes had competed in this event, as well as many others.

"Are you done, Mommy?" Emily danced around among the stones, her impatience obvious. "Jemmy and I want to play basketball."

"Just about." Olivia motioned to the manager. "These two, please."

She paid for them and waited while he and his helper hoisted them into a wheelbarrow and loaded them into her car. One more errand at the grocery store and they were on their way back, with Albert's house their first stop. She wasn't surprised to find Will and Jemmy outside with the puppies, who were getting big enough to scamper around the grassy lawn.

"Em'ly!" Jemmy hollered as he ran toward the car before it stopped.

Gasping, Olivia slammed on the brakes.

"Whoa, pal." Will scooped him up and walked over to the driver's side. "Hi, neighbor. What brings you to this side of the fence?"

"I need some muscle. Think you can haul those rocks out for me?" She hooked her thumb over her shoulder, then climbed out, with Emily scampering out on her own.

After setting Jemmy down, Will moved to the back of the car and opened the hatchback. "Whew. I don't know. Didn't have my spinach yet today."

She laughed. "Well, Popeye, maybe you can just shove them out onto the ground. We'll have my boulder fumble over here on the lawn—" she walked to the grassy part of the yard "—so we can just leave them here until the real athletes arrive."

"Oh, now you've done it. Can't let that go unchallenged." He reached into the back and maneuvered the largest stone to the edge, then hefted it. His bulging biceps strained the sleeves of his T-shirt, but no pain showed on his face. "Now, where did you say you wanted this?"

"Down. Just down." *Oh, my, he was strong.*

"You sure?" He just stood there grinning, almost challenging her.

"Well, then, how about over by the fence."

He strode in that direction, barely huffing with his load. Her own breathing hitched up a bit as she observed this display of strength.

"No, that won't do. Take it over by the old well." The well had been filled in, but its round stone wall remained. She would plant some pansies or petunias there once she owned this property.

Will walked that way.

"No, wait." This was fun. "Over by the house."

His stride barely slowed.

"No, that won't do, either." Olivia was running out of ideas. "Just bring it back over here." She motioned toward the grass.

He complied.

"Okay, you can drop it now, Popeye. But don't forget to eat your spinach."

He casually squatted to set down the stone rather than drop it, then retrieved the smaller one from the car and put it beside the big one. "Anything else?"

"Well, clearly, I didn't buy a big enough stone for the real athletes." To cover her silly breathlessness, she forced out a laugh. "Should have taken you along to find one you couldn't carry so easily. If all the men can do that, it won't be much of a competition."

"Yeah, but if the competitors have to run, it'll be harder. This one should work fine." He patted her shoulder, and a pleasant sensation streaked up her neck.

She made the mistake of looking up into those stunning blue eyes, and the nice feeling raced down to her heart. She huffed out another laugh. "If you say so."

She needed to get away from him before… "Emily, let's go fix lunch for Granddad and Miss Nona." The children had been occupied with the puppies, so they hadn't noticed this little "boulder fumble."

"Can Jemmy come?"

"No." She didn't mean to sound sharp, but somehow she had to rebuild her defenses against Will's all-too-manly appeal. "I'm sure Mr. Will has plans, and so do we."

She made the mistake of looking back into those blue eyes. He winked.

Of course, he did.

"Okay, then. See you later." That devastating smile in place, he stepped back as though releasing her.

She drove around to her own driveway, determined to put Will Mattson out of her thoughts. But her mind kept returning to the sight of him casually carrying that heavy stone as though it was a bag of feathers. Not only did she admire his physical strength, but she also enjoyed his sense of humor. She could see spending more time with him and maybe not just because of the children. Would he enjoy the Santa Fe Opera? Or would the rodeo next week be more his speed? They could take the children to the rodeo and...

What was she thinking? She couldn't let Will get under her skin this way. But how could she stop it when she, like Alice, kept sliding farther down the rabbit hole?

Watching across the pastures, Will followed Olivia's progress along the road to her house. She sure was fun to joke around with, but it had taken all the grit he could muster to act like that stupid rock wasn't heavy. Right now, his arms, his back, and even his legs ached. Man, he needed to get back to the gym and resume his strength training. He hadn't worked out, other than chopping wood for Albert, since taking on Jemmy's care. He wouldn't change that for the world, but he also needed to take care of himself. Maybe tomorrow, he'd take Jemmy to the gym and show him how it was done.

Or maybe he could ask Olivia to babysit while he went to work out. Dropping Jemmy off and picking him up would give Will more time to spend with her and explore these feelings he couldn't dismiss. Or maybe he should invite her and Emily the next time he went to Santa Fe.

That was it. He'd invite them to the rodeo in Santa Fe next week. She could probably use a break from their competition as much as he could.

That afternoon, while Jemmy napped, he moved the woodpile to the back of the house so it wouldn't be in the way of the festivities in another three weeks. The activity gave him some exercise and reinforced his resolve to get back to the gym.

"Hey, Popeye!" Olivia called to him over the stone fence separating the properties. "Didn't get enough strength training this morning?"

His heart kicked up. *Invite her now.* He sauntered over and leaned his elbows on a smooth spot on the rough stone top. "Hey, what are you up to this afternoon?" *Duh!* Stupid question. The watering can she held obviously meant she was tending the flowers growing along the house's back path.

She grinned as though she could read his mind. And it was a friendly smile, not reserved, like the ones she'd given him so often in the past. "Hey, I noticed Pecky's out in the yard with the other chickens. Is she okay?"

"Seems to be." Will grunted. "And a good thing, too. She laid her first egg the other day…in Jemmy's shoe. He didn't notice when he went to put it on and stepped on it."

"Oh, dear." Olivia winced. "What a mess."

"Yeah." He chuckled. "That's when he decided to try her again in the yard. With all the other baby chicks hatched, she's not the youngest anymore." He glanced toward the flock. "They're all getting along pretty well."

"I'm so glad. I can see how taking care of her was good for him, but now that he has Buddy, he still has an important responsibility."

"Right." He gave her his friendliest smile. "Say, I was just thinking. You and Emily want to go to the Rodeo de Santa Fe next week? I think the kids would really like it."

Her eyes widened and her jaw dropped. "I was just going to ask you the same."

"Great minds."

She laughed, that musical sound that he could listen to all day. "If not great, at least on the same track." She tilted her head toward Albert's house. "About some things."

"Right." He couldn't let this conversation turn antagonistic. "This would be Jemmy's first rodeo. He liked riding your horse, so this would be the next step in turning him into a gen-u-ine cowboy." He grinned.

She rolled her eyes, but returned one of her beautiful smiles. "Emily loves rodeos. I think she'd like to be a barrel racer."

"How do you feel about that?"

She shrugged. "I don't know. We'll have to see. An important part of homeschooling is teaching a child all the options out there and trusting the Lord to guide them to the career He wants for them."

"Sounds good. And I look forward to learning more about this homeschool thing." He was glad for this insight into her spiritual life. It wasn't always easy for him to trust the Lord with Jemmy's future. How much harder it must be for a widow to trust Him. "So. Rodeo?"

"Sounds good."

He chuckled at the way she echoed his words. So much to like about this lady. If it wasn't for their dispute over who got to buy Albert's place, he wouldn't hesitate to let himself fall for her.

Who was he kidding? He already stood on that precipice, and only one small bump, or rodeo, might send him over the edge.

Chapter Eleven

Popcorn and soda in hand, Olivia used her elbow to gently guide Emily to her seat beside Jemmy in the bleachers six feet above the rodeo arena. On Jemmy's other side, Will helped his nephew get settled. Over their kids' heads, he gave her his winning smile. Or maybe he was just as excited to be here as she and the kids were.

"Can you see okay?" He winked.

"Perfectly." She laughed at his silly question. They'd scored seats in the front row, right across the arena from the chutes.

As noisy attendees filled the stands, Jemmy stared around at the crowd, but he seemed more curious than alarmed. Although she hadn't known him very long, she could see this was progress.

Before the main rodeo began, little cowboys wearing helmets rode sheep around the arena for the mutton-busting competition. Olivia watched Jemmy as he stared wide-eyed at boys not much older than he was trying to hang on to the wooly beasts. Was he thinking he could do that, too? That would be a bold move for him.

Next came the rodeo queens riding at breakneck speed around the arena perimeter, some carrying flags and others waving to the crowd. Emily jumped out of her seat and waved furiously as they flew past. Miss Rodeo America, on her beautiful palomino, rode to the center of the arena carrying the American flag while a local high school girl sang "The Star-Spangled Banner." The announcer offered a prayer for the safety of all participants, and the rodeo began...with a bang.

When the first Brahma bull burst from the chute and tried to throw its rider, Olivia checked the kids for their reaction. Emily was fine. After all, this was not her first rodeo. She chuckled at the pun. Before she could share it with Will, she saw Jemmy hiding his face in Will's shoulder as the bull jumped and twisted violently, trying to throw its rider.

"It's okay, pal." Will pointed to the action. "Just watch."

After the cowboy managed to hang on for the requisite eight seconds, a horn sounded, and he jumped off and ran toward the fence, the bull right on his heels.

Jemmy cried out, and Emily grabbed his hand. "It's okay! Watch the clowns."

Dressed in baggy, mismatched clothes, the rodeo clowns diverted the bull's attention until the cowboy could climb the fence to safety.

"See." Emily giggled, and Jemmy joined in laughing at the clowns' silly but lifesaving antics.

After a moment, Jemmy appeared thoughtful. "Unka Weeoo, are you a weal cowboy? Why don't you wide the bulls?"

Will snorted out a laugh, then seemed to force the grin from his face. "Want some more popcorn, pal?"

This was too good to pass up. "Yes, Uncle Will." Olivia gave him a teasing smirk. "Why don't you ride the bulls?"

"Hey, whose side are you on?" He returned a playful

scowl. Then to Jemmy, he explained, "Those guys are a special breed, pal. Not every cowboy is cut out to ride bulls. Just wait until you see the steer wranglers. That's more my speed."

From that moment, Jemmy settled down to enjoy the various events, even the bucking broncos. With every event, Will looked her way as though checking to see that she was enjoying the rodeo as well. She returned a smile to assure him that she was.

"Mommy, I want to be a barrel racer." Emily skipped along beside Olivia as they made their way through the crowded parking lot after the final event. "I want to carry the flag."

"That would be exciting, wouldn't it?" Olivia would explain later that the rodeo queens who raced around the perimeter of the arena, carrying flags that streamed above their heads, weren't always barrel racers, too.

Beside them, Will held Jemmy's hand as they walked. "How about you, Jemmy? What did you like the best?"

"The clowns." Jemmy looked up at Will for approval.

Olivia and Will traded one of their frequent looks and smiles.

"I like the clowns, too," Emily said. "They're silly."

Olivia took in Will's Western garb. As always, he sure did look like a cowboy. "Did you ever take part in a rodeo event?"

"Not formally. I did spend several summers at the Double Bar M and got pretty good at roping and reining. Those are parts of real-life cowboy work." He chuckled. "Even got to help gentle a couple of mustangs. That was like riding a bucking bronco."

"Ha. I can picture that." Olivia gave him a little smirk. "Why don't you enter the rodeo?" Not that she wanted him to, but it was fun to tease him. "Surely you're not too old to start."

"Ha, yourself." Will lifted Jemmy and swung him around on his back. "I would take you up on your invitation to ride Dawson."

"Just name the day." The thought of riding Fred beside him gave her a sweet longing.

"I'll do that." He glanced over his shoulder. "Hey, pal, how about riding a bucking bronco?" He jogged around in a small circle.

Jemmy flung his arms around Will's neck, his eyes wide with terror.

"Wait, Will. He's scared. Let him down." Olivia reached for the boy...just as he started to squeal with delight.

"Giddyap." He bounced in the loops of Will's arms, and they jogged the rest of the way to the truck, with Olivia and Emily chasing behind.

"Barbecue?" Will asked her as he buckled Jemmy into his car seat.

"Sounds good."

In fact, everything sounded good these days when it came to time spent with Will and Jemmy. Including the country songs they sang along to with the radio on the way home from their roadhouse supper.

As she tucked Emily into bed, her daughter gazed up at her with sweet innocence shining in her brown eyes. "Mommy, why can't we live with Jemmy and Mr. Will? That way we could both have the puppies all the time."

Tonight it was Jemmy's turn to keep them.

"Well, sweet pea, we're not really a family—"

"We are. We do everything together. It would be fun to be in the same house."

Olivia kissed her forehead. "Good night, dearest." She walked to the bedroom door, where Dad waited.

"Livy, I want to talk to you, if you're not too tired."

"Sure."

Walking without his cane, which he'd been doing since last week, Dad settled at the kitchen table. "I, uh, I'm not sure how to say this, but, well—"

"You're in love with Nona." Olivia's heart dipped, then shot upward. She grasped his hand across the table. "Oh, Dad, I'm so happy for you."

He chuckled. "Can't keep any secrets from you."

"Have you told her?"

Again, he laughed. "She told *me*. Said at our ages—well, she's still a spring chicken compared to me—we shouldn't waste any more time before shedding the loneliness we've both felt since our spouses died."

Olivia winced inwardly. How well she knew that same aching loneliness even a loving family couldn't soothe away. "Well, good for her. And good for you. What are your plans?"

"Still working on that. Once she finishes her book and we get past the Fourth of July—" he gave her a meaningful look "—we'll see what's what."

Olivia squeezed his hand. "I'll be praying for you." And praying for herself and Emily now that one more challenge to their future had arisen. If Dad married Nona and moved to Florida, how could she manage to run this place by herself? Or maybe Nona and her two daughters would want to live here. That would mean Olivia needed Albert's house more than ever.

* * *

The next day, Will took her up on the invitation to ride her horses. She and Emily found him at the shed getting ready to teach Jemmy how to saddle Dawson while the little guy sat on the nearby bale of hay. Both were dressed in jeans and Western shirts, with their Stetson hats completing the picture of two cowboys. Emily parked herself beside Jemmy.

"First the saddle blanket." He held it out and let the kids feel the heavy wool fabric. "This protects the horse's back from rubbing by the saddle." He nodded to Olivia. "Hey." His gorgeous smile sent a tickle through her heart.

"Hey, yourself. You sure you want to ride Dawson? He can be a little frisky." She wouldn't advise putting Jemmy on her younger gelding, but she'd wait to see what he planned.

"Just want to try him out. Fred's a little tame for me." He glanced at Jemmy. "Next, the saddle."

His muscular arms rippled as he easily hefted the adult-size saddle onto Dawson's back. Olivia took a deep breath and looked away from the all-too-appealing picture.

"Make sure it's set right so he'll be comfortable, then reach under his belly and grab the cinch." He followed through with the rest of the procedure, adjusting the bit in Dawson's mouth and checking the length of the reins. "Okay, Jemmy, I'm gonna take a little ride around the pasture. You stay right here with Emily and Miss Olivia." He looked at Olivia, eyebrows raised as though asking for her agreement.

She returned a nod. "We'll be right here."

After adjusting his hat, he led Dawson from the shed and mounted him. As expected, the gelding turned around, trying to return to his stall.

"Hey, now, boy. Wrong direction." Using his voice, knees and the reins, Will straightened Dawson's heading and tapped his heels into the horse's sides. Olivia could sense every command. This cowboy knew his stuff. With a toss of his head as his last resistance, the gelding took off in a canter across the small pasture.

Olivia could see the kids were enjoying the show, maybe remembering the fun they'd had at yesterday's rodeo. "Want to ride?"

"Yes!" Emily jumped up and headed toward Will, who was on the other side of the pasture, putting Dawson through his paces.

"Not so fast." Olivia grabbed her shirt. "I meant on Fred."

Emily slumped her shoulders comically. "Aw, Mom." Then she brightened. "Come on, Jemmy. Let's saddle good old Fred."

Soon they were mounted on the reliable older gelding and having the time of their lives as Olivia trotted them around the pasture. She hadn't felt this much freedom and unbounded joy since Sancho was still alive.

The next day, Olivia and Emily rode with Will and Jemmy to church, which was becoming an enjoyable habit. They left the kids in June's Sunday school class and attended Will's singles class. Several of the young women gave her the side-eye, but for the most part, everyone was friendly. She did catch two of the young men giving her a once-over, but apparently being with Will Mattson made her off-limits. It felt so strange to be among singles again. That was where she'd met Sancho. Yet, somehow, the memory didn't sting as much today.

After the lesson, they picked up the kids and headed

toward the sanctuary. Once again, Olivia had that warm feeling that was becoming so comfortable. Maybe Will would take them all to lunch, since the puppies had begun to eat puppy mix and had plenty of water in their kennel. If not, she would invite him and Jemmy to share her leftover meat loaf. Whichever way it happened, she only knew she wanted to spend this Sunday with Will.

Was that good or bad? Safe or dangerous? She had no idea.

After Sunday school, Will ushered Olivia, Emily and Jemmy into a back pew beside Aunt Lila Rose and her boys. Greeting his aunt with a hug, he took in her weary expression. "You look like you could use a break. Why don't I take the boys this afternoon so you can have some 'me' time?"

She breathed out a long sigh. "That would be wonderful. My friends have been asking me to go for lunch with them for weeks now. It'll be nice to finally accept."

"Tell you what. You hitch a ride with one of them, I can use your van to cart the boys out to Albert's place and Olivia can drive my truck." He glanced at Olivia for the expected approval, only to see her face registering shock. A sinking feeling lodged in his chest. "Um, well, maybe—"

"Sure. Yes." She offered a smile that looked more like a grimace. "I'll be glad to drive."

During the service, he looked her way several times, but she seemed to avoid him. Had he made a terrible mistake expecting her to help with the boys? Had he ruined their budding friendship by making an assumption? Or was she just paying attention to Pastor Tim's sermon? Which was what he should have been doing.

Lord, please don't let me blow this. I've gotten used

to Olivia being in my life, and want to be more than just friends with her. But I know You've given me a mission to help Aunt Lila Rose raise these boys. How can I figure out what to do?

As he prayed, the thought came to him. Maybe this afternoon he'd find out Olivia really couldn't deal with the boys the Lord had put in his care. If so, then after Albert's birthday bash, he'd have to pull back from spending so much time with her. And that would rip his heart right out of him.

But what if she discovered she actually enjoyed being with the boys? That would change everything. *Lord, You know what's best, but please change her heart toward these little guys.*

As usual, drive-through was the solution for lunch. Will drove the van, and Olivia his truck. When he saw how well she handled the vehicle, he second-guessed his idea of distancing himself from her. What was not to like about this lady? Nothing.

Back home, or his soon-to-be home, he expected her and Emily to go over to her place. Instead, they both helped him carry the bags of burgers and fries into Albert's house and set everything out on the dining-room table. The old gentleman was glad for the company.

With everyone seated, Will offered a blessing. He breathed a sigh of relief when the boys put on their best manners. Well, except for the faces they made at each other across the table and their silly knock-knock jokes. At least they didn't throw french fries at each other.

"Knock, knock," Benji, the usual ringleader, challenged Jeffie.

"Who's there?"

"Auto."

"Auto who?"

"You auto know it's me by now."

The boys giggled, as did Emily. Even Olivia chuckled. Will could see a softening in her face as she looked at the boys. It was the same way she looked at her own daughter and Jemmy. Surely she could see these boys weren't the hooligans she'd imagined them to be.

"Okay, I've got one, Benji." Olivia smiled at him. "Knock, knock."

Will didn't hear the rest of her joke for the thumping of his heart. All he knew was that she wasn't just tolerating his boys, she was engaging with them. That didn't mean she wanted to be fully involved in their upbringing, but it was a start.

Thank You, Lord.

Olivia joined the fun as Will and his boys played tag football. She'd played on the volleyball team in high school, so she knew the value of team sports in developing character and sportsmanship. She and Emily had changed into jeans and T-shirts, but Emily preferred to play basketball with Jemmy rather than rough-and-tumble football.

She watched as Will made sure each boy had a chance to carry the ball over the imaginary goal line, reminding her of the way Sancho never let any of his boys feel left out. And, like Sancho, Will was made for this life. His generous, loving ways warmed her heart…against her better judgment. But now, she could see that judgment had been faulty, born of grief over Sancho's senseless murder by gang members. These boys weren't hardened to life yet, and Will was doing all he could to prevent that from happening.

The highlight of the afternoon came about when Will

brought the six-week-old puppies out for the boys to meet and play with. The adorable fur balls soaked up the attention. Jemmy jumped into the middle of the fun, lecturing in his four-year-old way about how to take care of the pups. None of the other boys had ever had a pet, so this entire experience delighted them.

Olivia looked at Will, whose eyes were suspiciously red. She felt a little emotional herself seeing Jemmy come out of his shell this way. And all because his loving uncle took on the responsibility of raising a boy not his own. How could she not care for this man? But would it come at the cost of losing her own dreams?

The Fourth of July arrived in all its New Mexico Land-of-Sunshine glory, with a bright sun above and a light breeze carrying the aroma of Papacita's smoked barbecue ribs and flank steak to every corner of the property, and probably beyond. Olivia studied the events layout with satisfaction. Yesterday, the equipment had arrived, and she and Will had directed their setups in the agreed-upon spots.

She looked up at the brilliant blue sky. "Lord, I've done my best. Please let me win this competition."

"Your will be done, Lord." Will came up beside her and nudged her shoulder. "Amen." Beside him, Jemmy held his hand, his eyes bright with excitement.

She looked up at Will's mischievous grin. "Humph. The Lord takes care of widows and orphans, so—"

"Exactly. That's why my aunt's orphaned boys need me to win."

"Right." She smirked. "And I'm so sorry you're going to be disappointed." Somehow her dismissive words didn't feel quite right. What *did* the Lord want from this competition? This day?

"And here they come." Will motioned toward the open front gate. "Let's go help Albert greet everybody."

Cars lined the roadway outside the fence, and families flocked in. Albert stood by the gate shaking adults' hands and handing out the gift bags to each child. Will had enlisted several of his teenage cousins to help with the various activities, which both eased Olivia's mind about everyone's safety and concerned her when it came to the voting. Could she disqualify them without seeming petty?

Also among the crowd were Will's aunt and her foster boys. The oldest boy, Benji, pulled a beach buggy loaded with Tupperware containers filled with cake and cookies. Unlike many of the other children, who'd scampered away from their parents toward the bouncy house and other games, Lila Rose's boys stayed close to her.

"Okay, you can go. Just remember to play nice." Lila Rose headed toward Olivia. "Good morning. Where do you want the cakes?"

"Hi. Welcome." Olivia pointed toward the portable flooring laid out next to the picnic tables and food trucks. "You can set up the cakewalk over there. There's chalk to mark the circle for folks to walk around. My old tape player will provide the music."

"Great. Come along, Benji."

"Howdy, Miss Olivia." The bright-eyed boy grinned at her. So polite, and apparently not at all cross that his foster brothers were already playing without him.

"Hey, there, Benji. How about I help your mom and you go play?"

He eyed Lila Rose. "Mom?"

She gave him a cheery smile. "Run along." She watched for a moment as he darted across the yard to join the fun. "Thanks, Olivia. He takes his responsibilities as the oldest very seriously, but he needs to play, too."

As she helped unload the beach buggy, Olivia digested this bit of information. How did this woman manage to teach her boys such manners? If they were this well-behaved all the time, maybe it wouldn't be so bad to have them living here.

What was she thinking? She had her own plans for this place. But she couldn't shake off the conviction Will's prayer had made her feel. *Yes, Lord, Your will be done.*

"Mommy!" Emily ran through the gate separating the properties, Dad, Nona and Ina right behind her.

Ina had arrived last evening and stayed with Nona in the studio apartment.

"I'll show you where we've set up your booth." Olivia led them to an open-air tent, where Nona's books and Ina's drawing supplies awaited them.

"Looks great," Ina said. "I'm glad you were able to get everything I asked for. Now, if I can just keep pace with everyone who wants a portrait."

"Mommy, where's Jemmy?" Emily tugged at Olivia's hand.

"Em'ly!" Jemmy ran to greet her. "Come play." He gripped her hand and pulled her toward the bouncy house, where June was managing the many children bouncing and squealing in the safely tethered structure.

"Look at them go." Dad chuckled. "When did that little guy become so brave?"

"Maybe it's because June's in charge." Olivia's heart warmed. "He's been in her Sunday school these past few weeks. And Will says Jemmy's decided Lila Rose's boys aren't too rough on him."

"I'm sure playing with Emily has helped, too." Nona watched Olivia's daughter with the fondness of a grandmother. "She's such a sweetheart."

"She sure is." Dad took Nona's hand. "Come on, darlin'. Let's get your books organized."

Her responding smile further warmed Olivia's heart. During these past days since Dad told her about his developing relationship with Nona, she'd grown closer to the author. Who could have imagined he would come back from the brink of giving up on life to discovering renewed energy after finding this dear lady to be his companion?

Several adults tossed beanbags toward—and sometimes *into*—the cornhole boards. Across the pasture in the archery range, others took aim at two straw targets painted with large bull's-eyes. In her own pasture, two young Mattson cowboys gave kids horseback rides on Fred. For the competitive events, Will had enlisted other relatives to judge the activities, so prizes could be awarded. Seeing him across the yard, she decided to confront him about their voting.

"It's nice of your relatives to come out and help. That'll give you some extra votes." She gave him a sassy grin, but behind her smile, a sense of unfairness lurked.

"Nope." He shrugged. "I told them not to vote."

She stared at him for a moment. "That's very sporting of you. Did you tell them what's at stake?"

"Nope," he repeated, then winked at her. "That's our little secret."

Whether it was his wink or his integrity about the voting or all the wonderful things she'd discovered about him, she knew in that moment she loved him. Alice had landed in Wonderland, and it wasn't as scary as she'd feared. If something more came of their relationship, he would be an amazing dad for Emily. What did it all mean for the future? Only the Lord knew. But she couldn't deny the love for him that continued to grow each day.

At midmorning, she corralled those who'd signed up for the boulder fumble on the lawn near the house. "Will, your name's not on the list."

Grinning, he shrugged. "Didn't want to show anybody up."

"Or be shown up."

"Hey, now." He winced comically. "Just being a good host."

A tall, brawny young man from San Juan carried the boulder with ease around the circular course, beating his competitors. A thirtyish woman from Riverton won the women's run. Even a few of the older children ran the course, carrying lighter stones to the cheers of the entire crowd.

At noon, the crowds lined up at the food trucks and bought fried chicken, turkey legs, french fries and ice cream. Olivia noticed the care everyone took not to litter, but to place their trash in the provided barrels. And their respect and deference toward Albert reminded her that she should get out of her own head more and try to befriend these same neighbors.

Throughout the day, guests paid a small fee to participate in the cakewalk, with the money going to charity. The music began, and participants walked around the circle, which was marked with numbers. The music abruptly ended, and Lila Rose drew a number from a bowl and called it. The person standing on that number then claimed one of the donated cakes. Would this be the favored event?

Enjoying the day as much as the guests, Olivia lost track of time. In the late afternoon, after Papacita declared the barbecued meat ready to serve, Albert gathered everybody, children included, and passed out ballots listing the various attractions. "Folks, I want you to mark your first and second choices for the events you like best. Everybody, children three and above included, can vote. Now, parents, you can help them mark their ballots, but don't try to influence what they vote for."

Once the rather chaotic voting was completed, he gathered the ballots in a pillowcase. "All right, folks, Jorge and I will go inside and count up these ballots to find out who—" he cleared his throat "—which event is the winner. You all line up and get your supper, and we'll announce the winner at the end of the evening." He and Jorge Lopez headed for the house.

Now Olivia's nerves kicked in. *Lord, please*...was all she could manage to pray. But when Will came up beside her and took her hand, she instinctively leaned into his shoulder, knowing somehow everything would be all right.

Will didn't know exactly when it happened. He just knew he'd fallen in love with Olivia. Maybe it was her obvious affection for Jemmy and the way she'd joined in the fun with the other boys. Maybe her silly, harmless teasing. Maybe her disinterest in his Mattson name and its social position in the community and beyond. Maybe his undeniable attraction to her many strong traits and virtues. No matter why or when, he had fallen head over heels for this woman. They still had some issues to work through, but some of them would be resolved this evening when he won the right to buy Albert's land. He would propose right away and promise he'd help her keep her business going. His law practice and his share of the Mattson legacy would provide enough income for both of them, but he understood her desire to have some independence. Maybe she'd be okay with having just one client at a time, as she did now.

"Folks, I see some of you have started eating!" Albert called out, interrupting Will's thoughts. "But let's take a minute to thank the Lord for the food."

Everybody paused while he lifted his face upward. "Lord of all creation, thank You for food, fun and friends. Thank You for health, even for old codgers like me." He glanced at Will and winked. "And thank You that You've already chosen the winners of tonight's games and…other matters. But we know that in You, we are all winners. We pray in Jesus's holy name. Amen."

"Amen," chorused the crowd.

A breeze sent the mouthwatering aroma of barbecued beef swirling around the yard, causing Will's stomach to rumble.

"Hungry?" He gazed down into Olivia's beautiful face, and his love intensified. It was all he could do not to tell her right away how much he loved her. How he wanted to protect her and Emily and to share life with them.

She returned a smile and, if he wasn't mistaken, he saw in her eyes a reflection of his love for her. Never had a lady looked at him with such genuine, selfless affection. Warmth and happiness spread through his chest such as he'd never experienced before.

"Sure." She sounded a little breathless, as though she was as caught up in the moment as he was. "Looks like Papacita and Lila Rose have the food line well in hand."

They located Jemmy and Emily and took their places at

the end of the food line. Folks loaded up a sturdy brand of paper plates with ribs, hamburgers, hot dogs, potato salad, baked beans and all the trimmings. They found seating at the half-dozen rented picnic tables or sat on blankets laid out on the lawn. Albert had hired a small band to provide music for the evening, and they struck up their first set.

"Livy, Will. Over here." Lawrence beckoned to them from one of the tables.

Once they'd settled the children and all began to eat, Lawrence cleared his throat. "Livy, we've got some news for you."

Both he and Nona focused on Olivia, who grinned broadly.

"Go on."

Lawrence gripped Nona's hand. "This beautiful lady has agreed to be my wife."

"Oh, Dad, Nona. I'm so pleased." Olivia's eyes shone with happy tears. She jumped up and ran around the table to hug them both.

"Congratulations." Will reached across to shake Lawrence's hand. As always, the older man's grip was firm and confident.

"This afternoon I emailed my book to my editor," Nona said. "So, it's time for me to go home. I've asked Lawrence to go with me so he can meet my family."

For a moment, worry crossed Olivia's face as she returned to her seat. She quickly brightened. "That's great. I can't wait to meet them, too." The worried look returned. "Um, Emily and I are leaving in the morning for the home-school convention in Albuquerque. The horses and the puppies…"

"No problem," Will said. "I'll still be here with Albert, so I can feed them and your hummingbirds."

Her happy expression returned. "Oh, thank you. That's such a relief. Hey, why not let Jemmy ride Fred again?" She laughed. "Turn him into a little cowboy, right?"

"Sure." He chuckled. "If he gets good at it and likes it, maybe one day he'll ride those bucking broncos."

With supper over, Lila Rose brought out her final creation, a huge sheet cake with ninety burning candles. "Time to sing 'Happy Birthday.'"

The crowd gathered around again and sang to their generous host. Some had brought cards and a few gifts, although Albert had told them not to. Even so, he graciously accepted a colorful patchwork quilt made by several of the ladies and a picture album of photos chronicling the history of his property. While helping Albert organize his clutter, Will had found numerous pictures from the past and had given them to a longtime neighbor, who put the album together.

With everybody's attention on Albert, Will took Olivia's hand and led her off to the side. "I—I, uh…" For some odd reason, the right words stuck in his throat.

"Yes?" She looked up at him with sweet innocence and expectation.

Now, he didn't hesitate. Tugging her into his arms, he planted a kiss on those beautiful lips. To his relief, she rose up on her tiptoes and returned the kiss. Will thought his heart might burst with joy on the spot.

After a moment, he pulled back. "I love you, Olivia. I want to spend my life with you."

She blinked back tears. "I love you, too, Will." She laughed softly. "Tried not to, but couldn't resist."

"Ah, won over by the infamous Mattson charm." He smirked playfully. "If I ask you…" For some reason, he hesitated to say "to marry me." "…do you think you might agree to exploring our…uh…friendship further?"

More tears. "I might agree to that."

"Oh, darlin'. You're too good to be true." He kissed her forehead and swayed to the music that had started up again. He sang along with the old love song, "Can't Take My Eyes Off You." She followed his movement, feeling just right in his arms.

The song ended, and Albert again called for everybody's attention.

"Folks, we have a few prizes to hand out." He held up a handful of envelopes. "The prize for the men's boulder fumble is Reggie Garcia." He went on to name the other game winners and hand each one an envelope containing a gift card for the local big-box store. "Now, you all voted for the best part of our Independence Day celebration. And our second place winner is Miss Ina's portraits!"

Will's heart hitched up. He hadn't considered how pleased the guests would be over getting a personalized cartoon drawing by a famous artist. Now, would his win for providing the popular food trucks, especially the one selling ice cream, cause him to lose Olivia?

"And our grand prize winner is…"

The band provided a drum roll.

"The bouncy house!"

Will staggered back as though a boulder had slammed him in the chest.

Chapter Twelve

The instant Will stepped back from her, Olivia missed the physical contact with him. It took her a moment to realize she'd won their competition.

"Oh!" She clasped her hands to her chest. "I can't believe it." She looked up at Will. His shocked, devastated expression shouldn't have surprised her, but it did. Only now did she fully comprehend what this loss would mean to him and Jemmy…and Lila Rose's boys. "Will—"

He lifted a hand and turned away.

"Will…" she repeated, trying again.

"Just give me a minute." He walked several yards away.

"Olivia!" Nona hurried over to embrace her, with Dad right behind. "I'm so happy for you. Once you remodel Albert's house, I'm sure we can keep it filled with plenty of artists who'll love this place as much as I do."

"Congratulations, Livy." Dad's tone held much less enthusiasm than Nona's. "You must be pleased."

She shrugged. "I'm sure it was the kids who voted for the bouncy house." She glanced toward Will and whispered, "He's taking it pretty hard." How could their relationship go forward now? How would she have reacted if he had won?

Following Will to a shadowed area behind the house,

she grabbed his hand. "Look, we have a lot to talk about. A lot to sort out."

"Yeah." He blew out a sigh so deep, she could feel it in her own chest. "Don't mean to be a bad sport about this, but…"

"You're not. You just had your plans, as worthwhile as they are, dashed to pieces." Why couldn't she just tell him right now she would let him buy the land? Somehow, the words stuck in her throat, maybe because it would be foolish to surrender her dream for momentary emotions.

"Listen, Will." She squeezed his hand, but he still wouldn't look at her. "I have to leave in the morning for my convention. When I get back, maybe we can sort everything out. If you want, I'll still get the kindergarten material we talked about for Jemmy. And—"

Now he faced her and gently grasped her arms, pulling her close for another kiss that made her knees go weak. He moved back and traced a finger down her cheek.

"I love you, Olivia. Nothing changes that." Even in the shadows, she could see his sad smile. "Like you said, we'll sort everything out when you get back. I'm staying with Albert until his grandson can get over here and help him move. Then I'll clear out so you can—"

"What part of waiting to sort this out don't you understand?" She grinned, hoping he could hear the humor in her voice.

He chuckled, but it sounded sad. He brushed a strand of her hair back from her face.

"Let's drop it for now." She nodded toward the crowd. "They're still enjoying the music."

"People sure aren't in a hurry to leave." He led her back into the lit yard. "Hey, look. Some of the guys are playing softball out in the field."

"Want to join them?"

"I could." He watched for a moment, then shook his head. "No, the kids are getting antsy, so I need to bring out our final surprise for them. Albert and I thought about having sparklers but decided against it because of the danger of sparking a wildfire. So, we bought glow sticks instead. Kids always like those."

He headed toward the house, and she followed. "Maybe we should have waited for the vote. The glow sticks would surely win."

He winced painfully.

"Too soon?"

"Ya think?"

"Sorry." She grasped his arm to stop him. "Will—"

"Shh." He brushed a hand over her cheek again. "Give me some time to adjust, okay?"

This time, she let him go. She had a few things to adjust to as well. Nona would soon be her stepmom, and her daughters the sisters she'd never had. The entire configuration of her family was about to change. At least maintaining her own business would help her keep some control over her and Emily's lives.

Who was she kidding? If she and Will decided to get married, they would have a Christian marriage, which meant both of them would surrender much of their personal control. And she couldn't think of anything better than being a wife to Will and a mom to Jemmy. Her marriage to Sancho had been a partnership, and he'd never bossed her around. Will would be like that. She'd seen it in everything he did and said. But, despite what he'd just said, she feared winning this stupid competition over who won the right to buy Albert's property might have destroyed her chance to find that out for sure.

The homeschool convention, set in the huge hospitality hall of a large hotel in Albuquerque, was the break she needed from the drama at home. She let Emily's interests guide which displays they visited and which videos they watched. Even if her daughter changed her mind as she grew older, this approach helped her develop discernment. The biggest problem Olivia had was keeping her mouth shut over some of Emily's choices. If she bought every book or teaching tool her daughter wanted, her budgeted money would be spent long before the week was over.

"Mommy, take a picture of the giraffe." Emily pointed to a tall cutout of the animal in a display for preschool books. "I want Jemmy to see it."

"Okay, sweet pea. Go stand by it." Olivia pulled out her phone and punched the camera icon. To get the whole giraffe in the picture, she stepped back several feet. Her heel caught on something, and she flailed her arms, trying to regain her balance, but found herself flat on her back on top of a flattened cardboard display. More stunned than hurt, she blinked as several people rushed to help. Heat flooded her face. How could she be so clumsy?

"Mommy!" Emily ran to her in tears.

"I'm okay, honey." Olivia tried to sit up.

"My dear," an older lady said. "You shouldn't move until the paramedics check you."

"I'm fine. Really."

Several others urged her to lie still, but she pushed up to a sitting position and pulled Emily into her arms.

"I'm okay. Just embarrassed. This display broke my fall."

Offering a sheepish grin to the crowd, she stood. "Not so sure about the display, though." She assessed the cardboard. "Maybe a little gray tape will help. At least that's what my dad always says."

Several people in the crowd chuckled as they dispersed.

"Don't worry about it." The lady who owned the display patted Olivia's shoulder. "I've been using this one for years, so maybe the Lord's telling me it's time to replace it."

Despite the lady's dismissive words, Olivia and Emily helped her put it back together as best they could. "Thanks. This will do for the rest of the week," the woman said.

"Mommy, did you get the picture?"

"Let me check." Olivia glanced around. "Where's my phone?"

After searching for several minutes, they found the device several yards away…thoroughly shattered. She must have flung it away as she fell.

"Well, that's that." She shrugged. "Sorry about the picture, sweet pea."

More than that, she wouldn't be able to text Dad or Will. Not that Will would want to hear from her after losing his bid to buy Albert's property. He asked for time to recover, and she could respect that. And Dad was probably having the time of his life with Nona.

She'd never been obsessed with social media, but it still felt strange to be out of touch. Borrowing a thought from the lady who'd so quickly forgiven her for ruining her display, Olivia decided to look for the good in this situation. Maybe the Lord took away her phone so she could better concentrate on Emily and her needs. She still had her credit card to make purchases, and she could always buy a disposable camera at the hotel gift shop for those all-important photos.

* * *

"I'm not saying you should be overly concerned, Joe." Will tried to keep the worry out of his voice as he talked on the phone. "Just that your granddad hasn't quite recovered from his birthday bash. You'd have been amazed at how energetic he was all day, but it's caught up with him. He's been down and out these past two days."

"Oh, man," Joe said. "I'm sorry work kept us from coming to the party, but we're having one for him when he gets here. Maybe I should come get him now."

"I think that's a good idea." Will considered his next words. "I guess he hasn't had a chance to tell you about selling this place."

"No, but that's okay. I have a buyer who's ready to sign and pay on the spot. He's a developer who's buying it as is because he plans to tear the house down and build a tourist getaway. I'm waiting for Granddad to get here to finalize the sale, but the guy's really eager." Joe sighed. "I'd have already signed, but I wanted to respect Granddad's dignity rather than sell it out from under him."

It took a moment for Will to swallow his shock. With his power of attorney, Joe had every right to handle all of Albert's business dealings. "Um, so Albert hasn't told you he planned to sell to his neighbor, Olivia Ortiz? He promised her she could buy it."

"Oh." Joe was quiet for a bit. "Is she ready to sign? Does she have financing? I can bring the paperwork."

"Well, no. She's out of town, but—"

"Look, I'm sorry to put pressure on anybody, but I've got things going on with my business that I can't leave for more than a day. And I need the money from the sale upfront to pay off the loan for the addition we've built for

Granddad. I need to take care of this now. If she can't sign and pay when I get there tomorrow, I'm gonna have to go with this other guy." He named the amount the other man had offered.

"I'll take it as is." The words came out before Will considered them. No matter how disappointed he was about their ridiculous competition, he couldn't let this place be sold out from under Olivia. "And I'll have a check ready for you." He had no idea what kind of financing she'd planned on, but he could use his own money and work it out with her later.

"That sure would uncomplicate things. So, we have a deal. See you tomorrow."

After disconnecting the call, Will felt a wave of satisfaction. He loved Olivia and wanted her to realize her dream. As disappointed as he was that he couldn't use this unique little ranch for raising Jemmy and Aunt Lila Rose's boys, he would do all he could to support her. What that meant for them when...*if* they got married, well, they'd have to figure it out when she got back.

He made sure Albert was settled in his recliner, TV remote in hand, then drove into town with Jemmy to arrange the cashier's check.

"Say, pal, you want to visit Benji and the boys?" Banking would be easier and faster if he did it alone. He glanced in the rearview mirror to see Jemmy's response.

"Benji and Jeffie and Mikey and Josh." His singsong recitation of their names showed his growing relationship with his foster brothers. He'd even endured a few bumps without complaint or fear as they played in the bounce house. "Em'ly's in A-bu-ku-kee."

Will chuckled. "That's right, pal. She'll be back on Saturday." And, if all went well at Will's adoption hearing the day after tomorrow, and if he and Olivia got married, they would be Jemmy's parents and Emily would be his sister.

The next morning, Albert was up early and feeling a little more like his spry old self.

"I hate to leave before Olivia and Lawrence get back, but I appreciate your taking care of the particulars on the sale." He took a bite of the scrambled eggs Will had prepared. "You sure you don't mind making trips back out here to tend the chickens?"

"Not at all." Will sat across from him. "Olivia's mentioned how much she likes having the fresh eggs, so I'm sure she'll want to keep them. And I have to feed the horses, too." And let Jemmy have another ride or two on Fred.

"I'm real pleased with the way you and Joe have taken care of this sale for Olivia." Albert eyed him for a moment. "In fact, you sure have been a good sport about all of this."

Will concentrated on his plate. He hadn't entirely worked through his feelings about losing out on buying this place, but surely the Lord had it all figured out. So much depended on what he and Olivia decided about their relationship. So much depended on the judge's granting him the right to adopt Jemmy, but that was no doubt a done deal.

Joe Winslow arrived from Amarillo around noon. Will checked for any problems in the purchase agreement and found none, so they signed on the spot, and he handed over the cashier's check.

"I'll take care of registering the paperwork," Will said. "We can take care of the rest through email." He'd have to wait for Olivia to return so he could register the deed in her name.

"Sounds like a plan."

With the sale in order, Will helped Joe load his pickup with Albert's stuff.

"I can't thank you enough for taking care of Granddad all this time." Joe reached out to Will. "It meant so much to him to stay long enough to throw that birthday party, but we never could have managed to come over here and help him with it."

Will shook his hand. "He's been an important part of this community for many years. He'll be missed."

"I was born here and lived here all my life," Albert said. "The neighbors were mighty kind to come out and celebrate with me, and I'll sure miss them. But my future's with my grandson and his family. I've got all my important papers and pictures, but you can help Olivia sort out the furniture and what all. What she doesn't want, you can donate to charity."

"Bye-bye, Mistuh Albewt." Jemmy hugged the old man who'd been like a grandfather to him these past two months.

Will had to hang onto his own emotions as they drove away. There would be a big hole in his own life now that Albert was gone.

After tending the chickens and packing up the puppies—who whined all the way to town because they didn't like being confined in the carrier—Will spent the afternoon at his apartment making sure he had all the information the judge might ask for tomorrow.

To his shock, when he and Jemmy went to the court-house, Grant and Mabel Sizemore sat in Judge Mathis's courtroom looking for all the world like decent people. Will had to swallow hard to keep from expressing his outrage. How did these two manage to fool everybody but him?

"Will, as you can see, Jemmy's aunt Mabel and her husband have joined us today." The graying, sixtyish judge peered at Will over her blue-rimmed reading glasses. "Like you, they are petitioning for custody of Jemmy."

Eyes wide, Jemmy stared up at Will and stuck his thumb in his mouth, a habit he'd given up weeks ago. Will gave him a reassuring hug. He'd brought him so they could celebrate after his adoption was confirmed, but the little guy didn't need to see this drama.

"While I appreciate your taking and passing the state-mandated courses to become a foster parent, as well as your prior claim to be granted guardianship of your nephew, I believe that a two-parent home is in Jemmy's best interest." The judge stared down at some papers. "Are you still living in an apartment?"

"Yes, ma'am." Will swallowed his rising panic. *Lord, help!* "But I just bought a house, and my girlfriend and I are making plans for the future. She's a widow with a daughter, and they've both bonded with Jemmy."

When he told Olivia he loved her, he should have proposed to her on the spot. Then he could honestly call her his fiancée. But he wouldn't lie to the judge. On the other hand, Olivia did agree to seeing where their relationship was going. Well, *might* see where it was going. Why hadn't he sealed the deal on the spot? Because he'd been too caught up in losing that ridiculous competition. And now he might lose Jemmy, too, because he hadn't put his love for Olivia above his disappointment over losing the right to buy Albert's place.

"Ah." Judge Mathis removed her glasses and leaned forward over her bench. "That does shed new light on the situation." She turned to Grant and Mabel. "I'm going to postpone my final decision until I can meet this woman and assess her qualifications. If nothing turns up to cast doubt on her, I will have to reconsider placing Jemmy with you."

"Now, Judge, don't you think we've already proved ourselves—" Grant bristled like a grizzly as he glared at Will.

"Now, honey." Mabel patted his hand. "You know Judge Mathis will make the right decision." She turned a toosweet smile on Jemmy. "I can't wait to be your mommy, darling boy."

Jemmy pressed against Will's side as tears slid down his cheeks. Only when they got back to the apartment and Jemmy sat on the floor to play with the puppies did he smile again.

Heart pounding, Will knew he had to solve this problem immediately. He'd tried to call Olivia right after his first phone conversation with Joe Winslow, but she hadn't picked up and hadn't responded to his message. At the time he hadn't felt undue pressure to explain in the message that he'd bought Albert's property, but would turn it over to her once they sorted out their plans for the future. But this new situation meant he needed to sort everything out right away. He punched her number's autodial and waited. No answer. Could she be mad at him? What for? She won the competition. Now he was mad at her. Why couldn't she just answer her phone?

Because if she didn't help him get through this minefield with Jemmy's adoption, maybe they shouldn't get married after all. Annoyed, he left a brief message about buying the property and said he'd explain the rest when she got home. He ended the call.

Wait. What had he just done? She'd need a better explanation than that.

He started to punch her number again, but it buzzed with an incoming call. He swiped to answer without even checking to see who it was.

"Olivia! Finally—"

A deep male voice sounded in his ear. "Sorry to disappoint, Will." He laughed. "Girlfriend problems?"

"Rob." Will slumped back on the couch. "Sorry. And, no—no girlfriend problems." Or none he could talk about, anyway. "What's happening?"

"Good news, bad news. Which do you want first?"

Will released a long sigh. "Bad news, I guess." He looked across the room to where Jemmy was playing with the two puppies. Would he have to give up his beloved little Buddy?

"You know we always keep DNA on all of our dogs. We're still haven't found Lady, but the DNA says the pups are hers."

"Oh, man…"

"And now the good news. For you, at least. The father shows as all-American mutt, so we won't be able to sell them as purebred or even a mixed breed."

Will heard the words but couldn't sort them out. "So, that means?"

Rob chuckled. "It means whoever stole Lady didn't want mongrels, so they dumped the pups. Though, how they planned to sell any of her pups without papers is anybody's guess. Maybe they were going to forge them." He paused. "So, if you want to keep those two little rascals, it's fine with me."

After a moment, Will found his voice. "Thanks. That's the best news I've heard all day."

"Anything I can help you with?"

Will considered unloading on his cousin. Maybe he'd do that later if Grant and Mabel were granted custody of Jemmy and Will needed some backup to prove they weren't as reputable as they let on.

"No, thanks. You've already helped more than you know."

Now, if he could just reach Olivia with this bit of good news, maybe his life would get back on track.

On the way home from the convention, Olivia drove to the phone store to switch her broken one for an upgrade. She'd wanted to increase her storage, anyway, so she was glad she'd paid for replacement insurance that covered most of the new one's cost. After the chunk of change she spent on homeschool supplies, her budget was already strained. The grocery store was her next stop before heading home.

It seemed strange to drive past Albert's place and not see Will's truck parked there. She'd said her goodbyes to Albert before leaving, but she could sense his absence, too. Now, to make plans for remodeling his house. She and Nona had discussed several great ideas. It would just be a matter of financing.

Her own house also felt empty. Since Sancho's death, Dad had been her rock, but his life would soon change. For the better, of course, but where would that leave Olivia? Would she and Will find a way to combine their goals so both could follow the Lord's plans for their lives? Or would he be too disappointed about not buying a refuge for his boys? Surely, there were other places he could buy for his aunt.

She and Emily pulled their wheeled suitcases into the

house, then brought in their groceries and bags of school supplies.

"Can I...*may* I read my new book?" Emily dug into her tote.

"Sure, sweet pea." She sat at the kitchen table to get acquainted with her new phone. Most of the buttons were the same, but she wanted to set it up with her own Wi-Fi and check for messages.

Once that was done, she checked her voice mail. To her surprise, Will had left several messages. She punched the icon to hear the first one.

"Hey, Olivia. I hope you and Emily are having a good time." Pause. "Soon as you can, give me a call back." Pause. "Love you."

Despite his sweet signoff, she couldn't miss the tension in his tone. That call had been five days ago. The second message said much the same, with a hint of annoyance coming through his words. But the third message cut straight to her heart.

"I bought Albert's property because Joe said—"

He bought the property? After their agreement that she had that right? A sick feeling rose in her chest. She swiped the message to delete it and the two that followed. If only it would be that easy to delete Will Mattson from her life.

Suddenly exhausted from her hectic week, she crossed her arms on the table and rested her head on them. What had she been thinking to let him get close to her and Emily? What could she do now?

A knock on the back door shook her from her stupor. That would be Will, of course. He had some nerve to come over here to gloat. She stomped through the living room and library, and flung open the door.

"What do you want?" She glared at him, just as she had on that first day when Albert had brought him over for an introduction. And just as she'd feared back then, he had used his lifelong friendship with Albert to wrangle his way into her life and steal her dream away.

And then, he had the nerve to stand there looking all innocent and confused, the only appealing thing about him the puppy in his arms.

"I, uh, first of all, welcome home." He gave her that dazzling smile, which now looked like a victory grin.

"You have some nerve." To her annoyance, hot tears filled her eyes. "What do you want?" she repeated.

Only then did she notice Jemmy staring up at her wide-eyed, clutching Buddy.

Will shifted awkwardly. "What's going on, Olivia?"

"You have the nerve to buy Albert's property while I was away, and you want to know what's going on?" She took Bitsy from his grasp and backed up to close the door.

He planted one dusty cowboy boot on the threshold. "Olivia, I explained—"

"Did you or did you not buy and pay for Albert's property?"

"Yes, but—"

"Case closed. Please move your foot so this door can also be closed."

His wounded look almost persuaded her to—to what? He withdrew his boot, and she shut the door. Through the glass, she could see sweet little Jemmy's tearful expression before they turned to walk away. Her heart dropped to her stomach. She'd bought several pre-K materials for him and even planned to ask Will if she could have him sit in on Emily's lessons. Thank the Lord that she learned the truth about Will's deceptive ways before their relationship got too far.

What was she thinking? It had already gone too far. She had fallen for him. Had meant it when she agreed to explore their relationship further. Even began to dream about their future together. Why hadn't she listened to her own doubts about him? Instead, she'd fallen for his charming ways and dazzling smile. Oh, and who could forget those piercing blue eyes? Ugh!

Now the tears came. She hadn't sobbed this hard since Sancho's funeral. Bitsy wiggled in her arms, and she set her down. After a few moments of self-indulgent crying, she inhaled sharply and headed to the bathroom to wash her face before checking on Emily. To her surprise, she found her daughter had climbed into bed fully clothed and was sound asleep. And no wonder, after their busy week. That meant she probably hadn't heard Olivia's conversation with Will. *Thank You, Lord.*

Poor baby. She would be devastated when she learned she could no longer play with Jemmy. But after Will's betrayal, how could Olivia have any association with him or his nephew?

She managed to put away groceries and partially unpack their clothes before tending to Bitsy. The puppy could now eat from a dish, so Olivia set water and food in the kennel in Emily's room. Physically and emotionally exhausted, with no appetite for supper, she followed Emily's example and went to bed. But weariness didn't make falling asleep any easier...or stop her tears.

Bitsy's whimpering and whining came from Emily's room and only added to her sadness. Poor puppy was missing her brother. How long before she got used to being the only dog in the house? Probably a lot sooner than Olivia would get over Will's treachery. The thought renewed her tears, and she finally cried herself to sleep.

In the morning, Olivia dragged herself out of bed too late to get ready for church. She hadn't wanted to go, anyway, since she wouldn't be able to avoid Will there. She managed to sort through the school supplies and set those she'd bought for Jemmy by the back door. Will's truck wasn't parked by his new home. Had he gone to church, or just not moved in yet? With him gone, maybe she should collect the eggs...

Oh, how annoying. She hadn't bought eggs yesterday because she was so used to getting them from Albert. But she would never step foot on that property ever again, so she'd have to give Emily granola for breakfast, though it wasn't her daughter's favorite. She'd make a trip back to town tomorrow for eggs.

And she'd stop by the home-improvement store for supplies to nail the gate between the properties shut. That should drive home her resolve to never speak to Will Mattson again.

That plan failed to give her the peace and satisfaction she'd hoped for. In the back of her mind, she couldn't ignore the thought that she should have heard Will out. But nothing could change the fact that he'd bought the house Albert had promised to her, the house she'd won the right to buy through their competition.

Wasn't that reason enough to shut him out of her life forever? No matter how much it broke her heart...and Emily's?

Chapter Thirteen

"The end." Will finished the final chapter of *The Fellowship of the Rings* and closed the book. "All right, guys, what do you want to read next?"

"*The Two Towers*," Benji said.

"*The Black Stallion*!" Jeffie shouted.

Will chuckled. Jeffie usually followed Benji's every move, so voicing a different opinion was a healthy step in developing his own identity. "Okay, you guys talk about it, and we'll take a vote tomorrow."

Why did he say that? The last vote he was involved in didn't go well.

After praying with the boys and putting them to bed, he had coffee with Aunt Lila Rose in the kitchen. "Thanks for letting Jemmy sleep over. I need to get to the office early so I can start making it up to Sam for all the time I've taken off."

She reached across the table and patted his hand. "I'm just so sorry for the way things turned out. I like Olivia, and I'm still not convinced she isn't the right girl for you."

Will snorted. "Well, she's definitely convinced she's not." He'd never seen Olivia angry until yesterday. Annoyed, yes. Indignant about the puppies being abandoned, yes. But all-out anger over his supposed betrayal of her trust and her refusal to listen to his explanation revealed an intractable side of her he didn't know how to deal with. He only knew he still loved her and prayed he could find a way to reconcile with her.

At least Jemmy had settled down after their encounter with Olivia. He'd been upset over her angry words, plus not getting to see Emily, until Buddy's antics diverted him. He'd even agreed to the sleepover with his foster brothers. This was a huge growth step, and most of it was due to his friendship with Emily. Maybe after spending more time with the other boys, he would forget the adorable little dark-haired girl who'd brought him out of his shell. And maybe, given enough time, Will could forget that girl's dark-haired mother…somehow.

With Emily beside her, Olivia guided the grocery cart around the aisles, finding more than just eggs to buy. She'd been so tired on Saturday, no wonder she forgot several staple items. She reached up to select a ten-pound bag of flour, then changed her mind and chose the five-pound bag. Dad had called last night from Florida to say he'd be there another week, so she would only be baking for herself and Emily. No more cooking for Albert. No more Jemmy gobbling up her cookies. No more enjoying Will's appreciative glances when he ate her carrot cake. And no additional hosting of clients beyond one or two at a time in the studio apartment. If Dad moved to Florida after he and Nona married, he would take his two pension incomes with him. Then how would she support Emily?

"Em'ly!" Jemmy came running up the aisle, arms wide.

Olivia's pulse kicked up. Where Jemmy was, Will couldn't be far behind. Instead, he was followed by Lila Rose's four foster sons and, several yards back at a much slower pace, the lady herself.

As Emily and Jemmy hugged, a lump formed in Olivia's throat. Oh, how she had missed this little guy. When he gave her a hug, she had a hard time holding in her tears.

"Miss Olivia." Benji grabbed her hand in an awkward but cute attempt to shake it like grown-ups did. "Got any more knock-knock jokes?"

The other boys crowded around and looked up at her expectantly.

She managed to hide her tears with a laugh. When had she fallen in love with the lot of them?

"Well, let's see." She struck a thinking pose, then looked down at the cartons of eggs in her cart. "Okay. Here's one. Knock, knock."

"Who's there?" the boys, even Jemmy, chorused.

"Omelet."

"Omelet who?" they all answered.

"Omelet you finish."

Their blank looks gave her another laugh. "Omelet? I'm gonna let—"

"I don't think they know what an omelet is." Lila Rose chuckled in her maternal way. "Guess I'll have to fix them omelets one of these days."

"Ah." A warm rush of affection for this lady flooded Olivia's heart. When Lila Rose and her boys moved out to their new home, they would have plenty of eggs for omelets. "Okay, here's another one. Knock, knock."

Again, the boys said simultaneously, "Who's there?"

"Cereal."

"Cereal who?"

"Cereal pleasure to see you today." And she meant it with all her heart.

This brought the desired raucous laughter from all the kids, including Emily.

"All right, gang." Lila Rose motioned them to gather around her, and they quickly obeyed. "You all have your assignments. Run along."

The boys scattered, with Benji holding Jemmy's hand.

"Mommy, may I go, too?" Emily's big brown eyes held a soulful expression.

Hesitating only a moment, Olivia said, "Okay. Stay close to Benji and Jemmy."

She chewed her lip and took a step to follow them. While she'd let Emily fetch groceries at Papacita's store, this was the first time she'd be doing it in a bigger store.

"She'll be fine." Lila Rose chuckled again. "The employees here know our kids and look out for them. A bunch of them are related to us."

Two months ago, Olivia would have rolled her eyes. Now, she could only feel relief.

"I'm so glad we've run into each other, Olivia." Lila Rose's smile disappeared. "I know you and Will had a bit of a falling-out, but I'm asking you to pray for him. He may lose custody of Jemmy."

"What? Why?" She'd never want that. Despite his buying Albert's land while she was away, he was a wonderful father to Jemmy.

"Jemmy's father's sister has petitioned for custody, and because she and her husband own a home and are already foster parents, the judge thinks he should be placed in a two-parent home."

"Oh, that's heartbreaking." Olivia glanced in the direction the children had gone, wishing she could give Jemmy another hug.

"Yes, well, Grant and Mabel Sizemore have a lot of people fooled, but—"

"Grant Sizemore!" Olivia gasped. "I know who he is, and I can't believe any sane judge would place any child in his home."

Lila Rose stared at her for a moment. "How do you know him?"

"Just look at this." She located the video on her new phone, thankful it had transferred from her old one.

"Oh, my word." Lila Rose gasped. "Please, you have to send that to Will."

Olivia hesitated. Would this just open a door she meant to keep shut? "Let me send it to you. You can forward it."

"Please." Tears shone in Lila Rose's eyes, and she grasped Olivia's hand. "I'm no good with these devices—"

"Mom, we got the spaghetti." Benji marched proudly up the aisle, followed by Jemmy and Emily.

"Good job." Lila Rose dabbed at her tears with a tissue as the other children rejoined them with their shopping treasures. She praised each one for getting exactly what she'd assigned.

Before she could think it through, Olivia tapped her phone screen to send the video to Will. She typed in: Ask Papacita for his CCTV of this.

There. That should do it. She wouldn't have to do anything more to save Jemmy from those horrible people.

But if that was so, why did she feel so melancholy when she hugged the boys goodbye, as though it was the last time she would see them, especially Jemmy? When she'd collected school materials for him at the convention, she'd envisioned the day when she would be Will's wife and Jemmy's mother. She'd mentally planned pre-K lessons for him and the lessons he could share with Emily. And now, that would never be.

Even today, as she watched these normal, healthy, rascally little boys help their foster mom with her shopping, her heart embraced them all. How could she begrudge them the wonderful home Will had bought for them? Was she being unreasonable? Or just disappointed that her own dreams would never be realized?

From the moment Albert had introduced Will—and his plans—to her, a tiny niggle of doubt about her own plans had tried to take hold in the back of her mind. She'd always shut down the thought because of her need to support Emily through her hospitality business. But what if having a father and brother were more important to her daughter? What if marrying Will and becoming a part of the vast Mattson clan would give her a supportive community she could always count on?

No. She could never marry a man who would betray their agreement. She would do all she could, even write a letter or speak to the judge in person about the Sizemores, to help Will officially adopt Jemmy. But she would never again trust him with her own future…or her heart.

Flanked by Ramon Martinez, Will strode into the courtroom armed for bear. If Olivia's brief video wasn't enough to convince Judge Mathis that Jemmy belonged with him, Martinez's CCTV and his testimony about Sizemore's thefts should seal the deal.

To his surprise, more than a dozen Mattson relatives sat in the room smiling and nodding their support. How had they found out about his adoption dilemma? Ah, well. In this small town, everybody knew what the Mattsons were doing. He greeted them with nods.

Rob stood and shook Will's hand. "We've all been praying for you."

"Thanks." Will swallowed sudden emotion and made his way to one of the front tables, followed by Martinez. At the other table, Grant and Mabel stared down their noses at him. He couldn't wait to wipe those smug grins from their faces.

Yesterday, he'd been bowled over when Olivia's text arrived with the ten-second video showing Sizemore forcing the boy to steal canned goods. Her unexpected help gave him renewed hope for their relationship. But when he tried to text back his thanks, she'd already blocked him. Stubborn woman. What could he do to make her listen to his reason for buying the land? And that he'd bought it for her!

One problem at a time. Right away, he'd contacted Martinez, who was all too eager to help him. Now today he had to convince the judge. Tomorrow he would try again with Olivia. Maybe this posse of relatives could help him with that, too.

"Mr. Mattson." Judge Mathis peered at him over her reading glasses. "I see you didn't bring Jemmy with you. Will you have a problem obeying this court and turning him over to the Sizemores?"

Will stood. "Yes, ma'am, I will have a problem. And I'm sure you will as well when you see this new evidence." He held up his phone.

"And this new evidence." Martinez stood up beside him and held up the tablet he'd brought.

"What new evidence?" Sizemore sneered. "We've already passed inspections and interviews. We've been foster parents for five years. What more—"

"One moment, Mr. Sizemore." The judge beckoned to Will. "Let me see what you have."

He presented his phone. "Just tap—"

"I'm not a dinosaur, Mr. Mattson." She glared at him briefly before tapping the device. "Hmm. The video is a bit shaky, and the sound isn't clear, but…"

"Your Honor." Martinez stepped forward and offered his tablet. "This will give you a better view."

She played the video, then motioned to the bailiff and spoke softly. "I want you to take Mr. Sizemore into custody for child abuse and a Class C misdemeanor of inciting a child to steal."

"Yes, Your Honor." The uniformed bailiff marched over to the table. "Grant Sizemore, I'm arresting you on a charge of child abuse and theft." He recited the man's Miranda rights. "Do you understand?"

Sizemore's jaw dropped and his eyes widened. "But— but…" As the bailiff led him from the room, he glared at Will. "This isn't over. I'll get—"

"That's enough, Mr. Sizemore." Judge Mathis banged her gavel on the sounding block. Once Sizemore was out of the courtroom, with Mabel following him in tears, she continued. "Now, Mr. Mattson, we still have the issue of providing a home for Jemmy. I will give you one month to improve your living situation. If you move into that house you purchased, I will let you officially adopt Jemmy. Then if you marry your young lady and she passes her interview, she can also adopt him. Until then, he may live with you." She banged her gavel again. "You're dismissed."

The room erupted in cheers as uncles, aunts, cousins

and various cousins-in-law rose to congratulate Will. Martinez clapped him on the shoulder. "I would be honored if you permitted me to cater your wedding reception. If you thought my barbecue was good, wait 'til you try the wedding feast I will prepare for you."

"Uh, that sounds nice." Will gave him a weak smile. This was not the time to tell his friends and family that Olivia wanted nothing more to do with him. In fact, there would likely never be a good time.

"Dad, you don't understand. He bought and paid for Albert's place while we were gone." Olivia held her phone away for a moment as she swallowed a sob. "What part of 'he cheated on our agreement' don't you understand?"

"Hold on. I think *cheated* is a pretty strong word." Dad sounded good, even over the phone. "Did he call and explain what he was doing?"

She sighed. "I dropped my phone and broke it on our second day in Albuquerque. Didn't get a new one until we got home. He'd left messages but didn't explain himself." She chewed her lip. "To tell the truth, I didn't give him a chance. Once he said he bought the land, I deleted his message. That was all I needed to know."

Silence on the other end.

"Dad? Are you still there?"

"Daughter, where's the good sense the Lord gave you?" He had the nerve to laugh. "You go right over there and ask him about it."

"But—"

"What are you afraid of?"

Good question. Was it fear of confirming his betrayal?

Or embarrassed pride over not giving him a chance to explain?

"And now," Dad said, "in other news. Nona and I are working on our wedding plans. Her girls are on board with our marriage, and I want you to be part of everything, too. Her younger daughter, Jillian, will be a senior in high school in the fall. Her other daughter, Maeve, just completed her BA, but her plans are up in the air. So, we all have a lot to figure out." Dad chuckled. "Livy, you're gonna love these young ladies. They're a hoot, just like their mama."

As he continued to describe Olivia's sisters-to-be, a sinking feeling settled into her chest. She and Emily had been Dad's world since Mom died. Now, other people were taking center stage in his life. She was happy for him, truly happy. But where did that leave her and Emily? While she'd been in Albuquerque, dreams of her own possible future with Will had balanced her concerns about the coming changes. Those dreams vanished after she'd listened to only a part of one of his voice mails.

The night of Albert's party, they'd agreed to see where their relationship was going. They'd also put off sorting out their different plans for the land. Why had she assumed he would agree to her establishing her hospitality business? Of course, he would still want the place for his boys. She'd just been too busy at the convention to think too much about it. Or…had she just been avoiding the truth?

Now, things were becoming clearer. She wasn't mad at Will for buying the little ranch. She was mad at herself because she knew he'd been right all along. The boys needed Albert's home more than any possible guests she might have, and even more than she needed to expand her business. The Will Mattson she had come to know and love would never do anything to hurt her. He must have had a good reason for his actions. And if at their ages, Dad and Nona could be flexible about their future together, she needed to be flexible about hers.

So, if Will wanted a life with her and Emily, she wanted him and all the people who came with him in hers. Jemmy and Aunt Lila Rose and all her boys and the entire Mattson clan, whoever they were. As for those boys, she might have to buy a book of knock-knock jokes, but she'd figure that out later.

Now, how could she make it up to Will for refusing to hear him out?

Easy. She gathered the ingredients for her carrot cake and got to work making her peace offering.

Will signed the stack of forms and legal documents his new paralegal, Lauren Parker, had put on his desk, then dug into one of his new cases, this one concerning an adoption. As he did for all his clients, he prayed for this couple, specifically that they would be able to adopt the infant left at the fire station where the husband served as a firefighter. While the mother hadn't seen fit to identify herself, at least she'd loved her infant daughter enough to put her in a safe place, where she would be found and adopted. And nothing gave Will more satisfaction than sealing the deal for such worthy couples.

Now, if only he could seal the deal with Jemmy's adoption. At least Judge Mathis had permitted Jemmy to stay in Will's custody until he worked out the problems regarding where they would live. He just had to figure out how to give his nephew two parents. Who could understand Jemmy better than he did? And Olivia had embraced the little guy with genuine love. She would make as perfect a mother to Jemmy as she was to sweet Emily. And Will had already started reading up on how to be a father to little girls. That was, until Olivia shut him out of their lives.

When he bought the place from Joe Winslow, he planned to sell the land to Olivia so she could establish her business. His loss meant he needed to find a house, maybe in town, for Jemmy and him. Aunt Lila Rose's three-bedroom home on a fairly small lot didn't have space for expansion, so moving in with her wasn't an option.

He'd gone into family law because of Aunt Lila Rose's work and his own family's dysfunction. He didn't want any child to go through what he and Megan had. Mom had left—he still didn't know what had happened to her—and Dad had withdrawn into his own little world, leaving the two of them to fend for themselves.

When Will was growing up, the only things that had made sense to him were Aunt Lila Rose's steady, loving guidance of her various foster kids and his time spent with his great-uncle Andy, who had taken him under his wing out at the Double Bar M Ranch. But Megan fell for a guy who, unlike Dad, seemed strong and decisive. Others could see Ed was a controlling narcissist, but Megan wouldn't hear it. Even before Ed beat her to death, then died in a hail of SWAT team gunfire, Will had determined he would do everything he could to protect Jemmy.

His work done for the day, he texted Aunt Lila Rose to say he was on the way. At her request, he stopped to buy some pizza makings, then helped her feed the gang their favorite supper. The boys, including Jemmy, had voted for *The Black Stallion* to be their next book, so he read the first chapter to them. They clung to every word as Alec Ramsay, a boy they could all relate to, went on his adventures with the magnificent stallion he'd befriended.

As always, he sat at the bedside of each boy and heard his prayers before tucking him in. Benji was the last.

"Mr. Will, when do we get to see Miss Olivia again?" He blinked sleepy eyes. "I've got some more knock-knock jokes for her."

Will shook his head. "I don't know, Benji. We grown-ups are pretty busy…"

"Is she mad at us?"

"No. Why would you ask that?"

Benji shrugged against his pillow. "When grown-ups get mad, they leave."

Will gripped his emotions so he could answer calmly. Like his own mother, Benji's single mom had abandoned him for reasons unknown. "Well, Miss Olivia isn't mad at you. She likes you a whole lot."

"When you see her, will you tell her we like her a whole lot, too?"

Will patted Benji's shoulder. "I'll do that."

As usual, Jemmy was asleep on the couch, so Will visited with Aunt Lila Rose in the kitchen.

"When will you see Olivia so you can give her Benji's message?"

Will gave her a mock-scolding frown. "You were eavesdropping."

"Guilty." She topped off his coffee. "Now, answer my question."

"I've already told you. She's blocked my texts and phone calls." At the memory, the day caught up with him, and he slumped in his chair. "I need to get Jemmy home."

"No, you don't." His aunt waggled a finger in his face.

"What you need to do is go out to her house and tell her why you bought Albert's place." She sipped her coffee. "I'll keep Jemmy tonight so you can go out there first thing tomorrow morning."

"Aunt Lila Rose—"

"Don't Aunt Lila Rose me." She held up one hand like a stop sign. "Just do it."

Irritated and amused at the same time, he raised both hands in surrender. "Okay. Okay. But I'm taking Jemmy with me so she won't throw me in the river."

He'd also take the paperwork from the sale and hand it over to Olivia as a peace offering, along with a promise to help her remodel the house to accommodate her future guests. If he really loved her—and he did—nothing would be too great a sacrifice to make her believe him. And after he got that settled with her, he would start looking for a bigger house in town, where he and Jemmy could live with Aunt Lila Rose and her boys. Maybe Judge Mathis would accept his aunt as the mother figure Jemmy so badly needed.

Olivia carefully took the carrot cake she'd made for Will from the fridge, placed it in her Tupperware carrier and snapped on the lid. If he didn't show up at his new home soon, she would pack up Emily and head to town to find him.

Last night, she'd kept watch for him, to no avail. Anxious to settle things with him, she'd prayed he would forgive her for not listening to his entire message. Prayed maybe they could pick up where they'd left off the night of Albert's party. Prayed she hadn't ruined any chance to make a family with him.

"Mommy, Mr. Will's here. And Jemmy!" Emily squealed with delight as she ran to open the front door.

While the kids hugged each other and ran off to play, Olivia could only stare at Will, her heart hammering in her chest.

"Hi." He gave her that devastating toothpaste-commercial smile and shuffled his feet like a schoolboy. "Got a minute?"

His shyness shocked her. When she could speak, it came out a whispered "Yes." She waved a hand toward the kitchen. "I made you a cake."

He blinked those gorgeous blue eyes, and for the first time since she'd known him, she saw a charming vulnerability. "You made me a cake?"

She snorted out a nervous laugh. "That's what I just said."

"Right. That's great. Thank you." He stepped over the threshold. "And, listen, I can't thank you enough for sending that video. The judge was about to give the Sizemores custody of Jemmy, but when she saw it, she was blown away. Had Grant arrested on the spot."

Olivia's eyes stung, and a lump formed in her throat. "I'm so glad. You're a wonderful father to Jemmy. It would have been a crime, literally, for that terrible man to get custody."

"You've got that right." He glanced down at the legal-size envelope in his hand, then held it out to her. "I brought you something."

"And that is?"

"Papers for you to sign so you can buy Albert's place."

"What?" She stepped back. "What are you talking about?"

"Olivia, I had to buy it or Joe was going to sell it to a developer. As is. Right away." His breathless rush of words hinted that he thought she wouldn't listen if he didn't hurry to say it.

Now, it was her turn to blink. "He was going to sell it? You mean he didn't ask Albert?"

"No. Once Albert gave him power of attorney, he was trying to do what was best for his granddad, which included building an additional room to his own house. He needed the money from the sale to pay for that, so he was ready to grab the first lucrative deal offered to him. He didn't know about our competition to buy the place."

It took a minute for her to digest this information. Finally, she said, "Well, that makes sense."

"I had enough savings to give him a check right away." Again, Will appeared vulnerable, almost apologetic. "I did it for you, Olivia." He held out the large envelope again. "The house and land are yours. And I'll help you with remodeling or whatever you need so it'll be just what you want for your guests."

Hot tears stung her eyes. Oh, how she had misjudged him, not only about his motives for buying the house, but also from the moment she'd met him. When her original negative opinion of him began to slip away as she got to know his true character, she should have known he would never do anything to hurt her. He truly was her knight in shining armor, rescuing her from losing out on Albert's land.

"So, do you want it or not?" He gave her a teasing grin.

"Yes." She snatched the envelope from him. "After all, we'll need a place for you and Jemmy and Aunt Lila Rose and her boys to live. I can't think of a better place than right next door. Can you?"

"No, but I—" He turned away and ran a hand down his

jaw, then faced her again. "You'd give up your dream for my boys?" He choked out the words, and his eyes turned suspiciously red, his deep emotion endearing him to her even more. "What about your plans?"

"My plans have changed from definite to uncertain. When I got the idea for entertaining artists, I was looking for a way to support Emily and myself, but that included having Dad's help. Now that he and Nona are getting married, I don't know what the future holds. He owns this house, and Nona loves it, so they may want to live here. If not, I can always keep on renting out the studio." She gave Will a sheepish smile. "Besides, there's this cowboy who might be planning to propose to me. If he does, well, I might just accept. So, there's that. I mean, if he actually proposes."

Will dropped to one knee and lifted pleading hands. "Mrs. Olivia Ortiz, would you do me the honor of becoming my wife?"

She swallowed her tears. "Yes, Mr. Will Mattson. I would love to be your wife."

He patted his shirt pocket. "Uh-oh. No ring. Maybe we could shop for one today."

"Unka Weeoo, you okay?" Jemmy appeared in the doorway, his blue eyes round with worry.

Right behind him, Emily looked just as worried.

Will stood back up and pulled Olivia into his arms. "Jemmy, I couldn't be better." He gave Olivia a quick kiss, then whispered in her ear, "We can improve on that later."

A pleasant shiver swept down her side. "Oh, you can be sure of that, Mr. Mattson." She turned to the children. "Who wants carrot cake?"

The now-grinning kids led the way to the kitchen table.

Once Olivia had served everyone a generous piece of the cake, Will took a bite and closed his eyes as he savored it.

"Man, this is good. You're an amazing cook, Olivia." He eyed the kids. "Jemmy, I have asked Miss Olivia to be my wife. Do you know what that means?"

Nodding, the darling boy gave him a crooked grin. "She's my new mommy?"

"That's right." He turned to Emily. "What do you think?"

"You're gonna be my new daddy?"

"Would you like that?"

She answered by jumping down from her chair, running to Will's side of the table and throwing her arms around his neck. "Yes, yes, yes!" She planted a kiss on his cheek as he returned the hug.

Olivia tamped down the sudden ache in her chest. Emily's memories of Sancho had faded over the past three years, and she didn't want her daughter to ever forget what a good, heroic man her father had been. But the Lord had brought Will into their hearts and lives to fill the void Sancho's death had created. She offered a silent prayer of thanks and released the ache to make room for joy.

Emily returned to her place beside Jemmy. "That means you'll be my brother."

"And you'll be *my* brother."

Olivia tried not to laugh, but when Will laughed out loud, she let go, too.

"Silly Jemmy." Emily giggled. "I'm a girl. I'll be your sister."

Jemmy twisted his face in confusion, then grinned. "Okay." He giggled. "Sissy sister."

"Baby brother."

"I'm not a baby," Jemmy protested.

"I'm not a sissy." Emily smirked, then giggled, as did Jemmy.

Will chuckled. "I think teasing is going to be a big part of their growing up together."

"I don't know whether to be glad I was an only child," Olivia said, "or sorry I missed out on the fun."

"My sister and I were relentless in our teasing." A brief shadow crossed Will's eyes, but he gave his head a quick shake and seemed to dismiss whatever sorrow that memory brought up. "Okay, guys...and girls—" He winked at Olivia. "We have cake to finish eating and eggs to gather. Then I need to get to work. Sam's been carrying my share of the load for quite a while. Jemmy, Aunt Lila Rose's expecting you."

"Let him stay here with us, Will," Olivia said. "It's not too soon for me to start learning how to be a mom to a boy."

Will gave her that smile she loved so much. "I think you already have the hang of it. Just stock up on knock-knock jokes, and you'll be fine."

"Right. Got it." Her heart flooded with joy as she anticipated a future that had been so uncertain only an hour ago.

Thank You, Lord, for answered prayer.

Chapter Fourteen

"Man, this is a real problem." Will studied the list he'd made. "Fourteen male cousins I grew up with who live in the area and another nine scattered around the country and the world." He scratched his jaw. "How's a guy supposed to pick a best man without offending the rest of them?"

Seated next to him at her kitchen table, Olivia viewed his list. "Oh, my. Please do me a favor and make a chart of all these names and what branch of the family they come from. And maybe put a picture beside each name so I don't embarrass you or myself at the reception."

He pulled her closer and kissed her temple. "Not to worry, babe. We're used to it." He glanced at the legal pad in front of her. "You haven't written any bridesmaid names."

"I don't have a clue about who to ask." She sighed. "I'm the only child of two only children, so I don't have any cousins. After I married Sancho, we got busy with starting a family and working in his ministry, and I lost track of my college friends. After he died and I moved here, I just didn't have a chance to make close enough friends to ask such a personal favor of." She snickered. "When I hinted the idea to Lila Rose, she shut me down real quick." She nudged his arm and gave him a teasing smirk. "Maybe I should ask Judge Mathis. She seemed to like me."

"What's not to like?" Will tapped her nose. "Once we get back from our honeymoon, we'll get those adoption papers signed and make you Jemmy's mom officially." It had been a proud day when the judge declared him Jemmy's dad, and he wanted Olivia to experience the same joy soon.

"Until then, I still need a bridesmaid." She gazed out the window toward the dozen or so hummingbirds buzzing around the feeder. "*Somebody* has kept me too busy to make any new female friends around here."

Will didn't know whether to tease or console her. He opted to give her another side hug. He wasn't sure a double wedding was the best idea, but he'd do anything to make Olivia happy. First, she'd wanted to elope, an idea Will liked a lot. Then Lawrence and Nona called to suggest they all get married together here at Riverton Community Church. As the only one who hadn't been married before, Will decided to go with the flow.

"Is Nona planning to have bridesmaids?"

"Yes," Olivia said. "Her daughters will share the honor. And Dad's asked Jim Wainwright to be his best man. Seems they got pretty close through their Sunday school class." She ran a hand over her blank page. "At least we know what Emily and Jemmy will be doing."

"Oh, yeah. Jemmy's excited about being our ring bearer. Emily?"

"She's excited about our matching dresses." She gazed up at him with those beautiful brown eyes. "And that's all I'm saying about it. You aren't allowed to see them until we walk down the aisle."

"I'm looking forward to it." Will planted another kiss on her temple. "You'll be the most beautiful Mattson bride in history."

"You sure about that?" She leaned against his shoulder. "That's a lot of history. All the way back to 1879."

"Ah, I can tell Lila Rose's been telling you about those thrilling days of yesteryear."

"Absolutely. You come from a long line of decent, hard-working cowboys. You should be proud of them."

He leaned back in his chair. "And still I can't figure out which one of their many descendants to be my best man."

"Here's an idea." She gave him that cute grin he loved so much. "What about Albert?"

Will stared at his bride-to-be. "Brilliant. Absolutely brilliant. We owe him big-time for introducing us." He paused. "You think he's up to it?"

She picked up his phone from the table and held it out to him. "Only one way to find out."

Standing at the back of the church, Olivia clasped Nona's hand as they watched her daughters, Maeve and Jillian, walk down the aisle in their matching peach satin tea-length gowns. Nona had generously shared her bridesmaids with Olivia, making their double wedding a true family affair. Ahead of them, Emily, also in an adorable white dress, dropped orange rose petals along the carpet. Right behind her marched Jemmy, in his dress cowboy suit complete with jacket and bolo tie to match his new daddy and carrying a white satin pillow bearing four rings...all safely tied on with satin ribbons.

Olivia wore an ivory lace tea-length dress, and Nona had opted for ivory satin. They both wore short, gauzy veils, secured by satin bands and layered over their up-swept coiffures.

"Ready?" Nona asked.

"Ready if you are." Olivia released Nona and clasped her bouquet of white roses with both hands.

The bridal march began, and the large congregation stood. The two brides walked side by side toward their respective grooms. Dad's friend and dear Albert stood to their right, completing the wedding party.

The ceremony passed in a blur for Olivia. For one brief moment as she recited her vows, she remembered doing this before. Then she gazed up at Will and knew God had sent him into her and Emily's lives. And what a blessing that Dad and Nona would still be part of their lives. Nona would continue to write her bestsellers, and Dad would manage the artists' retreat, only on a smaller scale than Olivia had planned. Will and Olivia had already remodeled Albert's former home to accommodate their own new family as well as Aunt Lila Rose and her boys. It would be a hectic household, but Olivia looked forward to the challenge.

At last Pastor Tim said, "I now pronounce you husband and wife, and husband and wife. Gentlemen, you may kiss your brides."

The sanctuary broke out in applause and plenty of cowboy-style yeehaws. Soon the two couples were cutting their twin wedding cakes, which would be served to their countless guests in the church reception hall. With Will having so many relatives, Olivia had suggested they post an open invitation. Papacita's lavish wedding buffet and the country band music filling the air meant everyone would have a good time.

"Congratulations, Will." Rob Mattson walked over, a glass of strawberry punch in his hand. "Miss Olivia, I don't know how my ugly cousin managed to win over a pretty lady like you, but welcome to the family. We're all glad you and your sweet daughter are joining us."

"Thank you, Rob." Olivia couldn't believe she'd ever felt disdain for this wonderful ranching family. And just maybe, she and Will would one day add their own children to its ranks.

"Now, how about you, Rob." Will nudged his cousin with his elbow. "When are you gonna get married? Those twins could use a mama, don't you think?"

Rob snorted. "It's not a mama they need, it's something to focus their energies on." He chuckled. "You're good with kids. Got any ideas for me?"

Will tsked. "Sorry, cuz. My expertise is younger kids, not teenagers." He glanced around the room and then gave Rob a sly look. "You know, my new paralegal is a single lady. How about I introduce you to her?"

Rob stared down at his wristwatch. "Would you look at the time? Gotta get back out to the ranch." He made a hasty retreat.

Olivia gave Will a sympathetic smile. "Guess we'll have to work on him. What's his story?"

Will sighed. "His wife, Joanie, died in an accident a few years ago. Took him a long time to recover—if one ever recovers from losing a spouse." He gazed down at Olivia, sending a pleasant jolt of love through her heart. "Sorry. You know more about that than I do."

She rose up on tiptoes and kissed his cheek. "But God can heal a broken heart if only we let Him."

"That's so true." He put his arm around her waist and pulled her close. "Are you having a good time?"

"Yes, indeed. You?"

He pasted on a fake frown. "You sure those kids aren't

making too much noise? I know you value your peace and quiet."

She watched the kids chase each other around under June's supervision. Although they were rowdy, they weren't destructive, just having their own kind of fun. Olivia didn't mind at all.

"Jemmy and Emily are having a great time. He's not so shy anymore." She chuckled. "Besides, peace and quiet are way overrated. There's nothing so sweet as the sound of kids laughing and having fun."

"I couldn't agree more." He squeezed her waist and gave her another kiss.

While she savored his sweet affection, peace and joy flooded her entire being. This was her new life, and she knew in her heart Sancho would approve.

* * * * *

Dear Reader,

Thank you for choosing to read *Safe Haven Ranch.* This story is set on a fictional ranch beside the Rio Grande near the fictional town of Riverton, New Mexico.

This book is a legacy sequel to my Love Inspired Historical novella "Yuletide Reunion," published in the anthology *A Western Christmas* (2015), and my follow-up novels, *Finding Her Frontier Family* (2022) and *Finding Her Frontier Home* (2023). In these stories, I created a family of five brothers who own and work hard on the fictional Double Bar M Ranch. Like any author who falls in love with her characters, I wanted to give each brother his own love story. Each one found his lady love and lived happily ever after. Now it's time to see what has happened to the descendants of these fine Christian characters. Thus, we meet modern cowboy Will Mattson and some of his many Mattson cousins.

Of course, literary characters need settings in which to act out their stories. My original inspiration for these ranch settings near the Rio Grande was my own sister's real-life tiny ranch beside that same mighty river. In my visits to her beautiful pink and historic adobe house, I was swept back into history, and my writerly imagination got busy creating characters to live there. Thus the Mattson legacy began... and continues.

I love to hear from my readers, so if you enjoyed *Safe Haven Ranch*, please write and let me know. Please also visit my website, louisemgougeauthor.blogspot.com, find me on Facebook at Facebook.com/louisemgougeauthor or follow me on BookBub at BookBub.com/profile/louise-m-gouge.

God bless you,
Louise M. Gouge